Georgie watched as he strode back out of the hospital entrance, the phone pressed to his ear as he chatted to his colleague, his long legs making short work of the distance to where his utility was parked in the hospital car park.

She let out a shaky little sigh and turned towards the lifts. A girl could get kind of used to having that heartbreakingly handsome smile bestowed on her every day of her life.

THE SURGEON BOSS'S BRIDE

BY
MELANIE MILBURNE

MILLS & BOON®
Pure reading pleasure

...A PURITANT A CYBER?

If yo... ...stolen property as a... ...reported un... ...d an... Neither the author nor the publisher ...r this...

All ...book have no existence outside the imagination of t... ...have no relation whatsoever to anyone bearing the san... ...They are not even distantly inspired by any ind...dual known or to be known to the author and all the incidents are pur...

First published in Great Britain 2008
Harlequin Mills & Boon Limited,
Eton House, 18-24 Paradise Road, Richmond, Surrey TW9 1SR

© Melanie Milburne 2008

ISBN: 978 0 263 86317 8

Set in Times Roman 10½ on 12¼ pt
03-0408-50331

Printed and bound in Spain
by Litografia Rosés, S.A., Barcelona

Melanie Milburne says: 'I am married to a surgeon, Steve, and have two gorgeous sons, Paul and Phil. I live in Hobart, Tasmania, where I enjoy an active life as a long-distance runner and a nationally ranked top ten Master's swimmer. I also have a Master's Degree in Education, but my children totally turned me off the idea of teaching! When not running or swimming I write, and when I'm not doing all of the above I'm reading. And if someone could invent a way for me to read during a four-kilometre swim I'd be even happier!'

To Rachel Mycroft for being a wonderful friend and confidante from the first moment we met. Some friends are pearls and change over time, but you are a diamond through and through. I value your friendship and miss you down here in Hobart so come back soon!

* * * *

A special thank you to Glen Hastings who gave me the idea for the opening scene of this novel and who also just happens to look exactly like my hero!

CHAPTER ONE

'HAVE you heard who your next registrar is yet?' David Lucas asked as he came into the doctors' room late on Tuesday afternoon.

Ben Blackwood looked up from the newspaper he'd been reading. 'No. I've been seeing private patients in my rooms all day. Anyone we know?'

The anaesthetist gave him a glad-it's-you-and-not-me look. 'Professor Willoughby's daughter,' he said, and seeing his colleague's grim expression added, 'I thought that might make your day.'

Ben tossed the paper to one side. 'So Daddy's little girl is trying her hand at neurosurgery, is she?' he asked with a little curl of his lip.

'Looks like it,' David answered as he poured himself a coffee. 'You'd better behave yourself, Ben. I know you don't like the man but his only child is on the training scheme and you have a responsibility to train her just as you would any other registrar.'

Ben got to his feet and gave his workmate a confident smile. 'You know me, Davo, I will remain professional at all times,' he said, pushing in his chair. 'It shouldn't be too hard. I bet she's short and dumpy and wears thick glasses, just like her pompous, overbearing father.'

David turned from the coffee-machine with a twinkling smile. 'She must take after her mother, then,' he said. 'I've heard she's a bit of a stunner.'

Ben rolled his eyes. 'Please, God, spare me from another female registrar who is more interested in how they look than how they learn. That girl before Matthew Chan was hopeless. I caught her checking her reflection in a bedpan, for goodness' sake.'

'Don't tell me the notoriously easygoing Ben Blackwood is starting to get a little tough on his registrars,' David said with a speculative smile. 'Or is it just female registrars you have a problem with?'

Ben gave him a quelling glance. 'Look, I couldn't help it if Phoebe Tatterton developed a ridiculous crush on me. God knows, I did nothing whatsoever to encourage it. She followed me around like a lovesick puppy. It was embarrassing.'

David gave a chuckle of laughter. 'What you need is another steady girlfriend, mate. What happened to what's-her-name?'

Ben frowned as he refolded the newspaper. 'Leila Ingham.' He brought his nearly empty coffee-cup up to his mouth and added, 'She decided it was time to find a nine-to-five playmate. I think she's seeing a schoolteacher now.'

'Oh, well, you know how it goes—one door shuts and another one opens.'

Ben looked back down at the headlines. 'Maybe....'

'Go easy on the registrars, Ben,' David said into the little silence. 'They're still learning. You were the same. Heaven knows, I was.'

'Yeah, well, my learning experience wasn't the same, actually,' Ben said in a weighted tone. 'I had to work hard to get where I've got. I hate it when these young people come in here and expect to be hand-fed all the time and get positive feedback on everything they do, including their stuff-ups. We're dealing with real people, not computer simulations you can reboot if you knock them off. Why the hell can't I get someone dedicated working beside me, instead of someone trying to prove something to her father?'

'You think that's what this is about?' David asked.

Ben ran a hand through his dark hair. 'I don't know... probably,' he said. 'Bevis Willoughby always had it in for me. He was a bastard from the word go. He used to single me out in tutorials, criticise me in front of patients and nurses—he even rejected my thesis research proposal. It was as if he was just hanging out for the boy from the bush to make a mistake.'

'Yeah, well, we all know what he was like around here,' David said. 'Thank God he's retired. I hated working with him, even though he was a damned good neurosurgeon, technically at least. But you really shouldn't judge the daughter on his track record. She might be completely different.'

Ben gave a little snort as he picked up his mobile phone from the table. 'Let's wait and see,' he said. Attaching it to his belt, he asked, 'Are we still on for a cycle in the morning?'

David shook his head. 'Sorry, mate. I promised I'd get the kids ready for school so Kate can go to her aqua-aerobics class. Do another twenty kilometres for me.'

Ben shouldered open the door with a grin. 'I'll do that.'

Georgie rushed back to her car from her early morning gym session, her hair swinging from its high ponytail as she threw her gym bag on the back seat. She glanced at her watch—if the traffic was kind to her she had forty-five minutes to grab a low-fat protein shake and get to the hospital in time for her first list with Mr Blackwood at Sydney Metropolitan Hospital.

She was excited and nervous at the same time about her

neurological term. It was a busy public hospital but she had heard nothing but positive comments about the staff and cutting-edge facilities.

She drove out of the car park and then realised she had left her mobile phone with the gym receptionist due to the new regulation restricting camera phones in the change rooms.

She parked again in the nearest space on the street and, turning off the engine, flung open the car door. But before she could even swing her legs out there was a loud *Thwack* and a very rude swear word cut through the air as a cyclist went sprawling from his bike right in front of her.

'Oh, my God!' she gasped, and jumped out to his aid. 'Are you all right?'

The man looked dazed and his arms and legs were bleeding from the scratches he'd received from his fall onto the rough bitumen.

Georgie mentally rehearsed the techniques learnt at the Emergency Management of Severe Trauma course she'd completed the month before. '*ABCDE—Airway, Breathing, Circulation, Disability, Exposure.*' She mouthed the words as she mentally ran through her priorities. '*First establish his airway with cervical spine control, then check his respiratory movements, then pulse and BP and stop external haemorrhage, then AVPU neuro assessment, then undress him...*'

Yep, airway clear, and he was breathing, she quickly assured herself. She unbuckled and pulled his helmet off and began inspecting the rest of him for injuries.

Ben opened his eyes wide as a touch as light as a feather skated over him. 'What the hell—?'

'Remain calm,' Georgie said reassuringly. 'I'm a doctor. Don't you dare move. I'm calling an ambulance.'

'I don't need a bloody ambulance, I'm a—' He frowned even harder. 'Hey, what are you doing?'

Georgie had already spied the mobile phone on his water-bottle belt, so she quickly took it off, dialled 000 and gave the operator exact instructions as to their location as she went to the boot of her car.

Ben shook his head, trying to get the school of silverfish that were floating past his eyes to disappear. In all the years he'd been cycling he had never once been knocked off by someone opening a car door on him, and it was a Porsche no less. The silly woman hadn't even looked!

'The ambulance is two minutes away,' she said, dropping to her knees beside him with what looked like a doctor's bag.

He watched as she began to rummage inside it, his eyes widening again as she brought out a hard cervical collar.

'Hey, I don't need that!' he said, trying to back away.

'It's a safety precaution,' she told him. 'You might have sustained a cervical fracture. You hit the road pretty hard.'

'Look,' he began again. 'I'm fine. I just—'

The sound of a screeching siren cut off the rest of Ben's words, not to mention the stricture of the collar around his neck. He lay back and grimaced as the young woman rapidly bandaged his scraped knees and elbows with enough bandages to make him feel like an Egyptian mummy instead of one of Sydney's leading neurosurgeons.

Georgie shone a bright light into his pupils, relieved to find they were both equal and reactive. She couldn't help noticing what dark blue eyes he had, fringed by long sooty lashes. He had a chiselled leanness to his features, his body toned and tanned, his unshaven jaw adding to his overwhelming maleness.

Focus, she reminded herself sternly. He might be super-fit and super-attractive but right at this moment he was a patient.

She took his arm, applied a tourniquet, and before he could protest through the choking cervical collar she warned him,

'This will sting a bit,' and had an IV line into his antecubital fossa just as the ambulance pulled up.

Once the paramedics joined in, Ben gave up protesting. He was placed on a spinal board with a sandbag either side of his neck, had a litre of normal saline running into his arm and an oxygen mask shoved over his face, pouring rubbery dry oxygen into his mouth and nose. After a final feeble attempt at freeing himself, he was loaded into the back of the ambulance, just as the police arrived.

'It was all my fault,' he heard the young woman tearfully confess to the officers, as the back door of the ambulance was slammed shut and the siren turned on.

'*Yep, it certainly was,*' Ben mumbled to himself as the vehicle accelerated towards his own hospital.

CHAPTER TWO

'NOT your usual mode of transport to work,' Rob Athol, the accident and emergency doctor, remarked dryly as Ben was unloaded from the ambulance. 'They phoned through and told us you got knocked off your bike. How are you feeling?'

Ben gave him a scowl as he ripped off the oxygen mask and collar. 'I'm perfectly fine, thank you,' he said. 'Some stupid girl flung her car door open on me. I was lucky another car wasn't coming.'

'You were lucky she was a doctor,' Rob commented, as his gaze ran over the bandages on Ben's arms and legs. 'It looks like she did a pretty good job on you.'

Ben gave him another furious scowl as he struggled out of the bandages, tossing them in the bin as he went. 'I'm more than half an hour late for Theatre,' he growled. 'And it couldn't have happened on a worse day. I've got a new registrar to train.'

'You sure you'll be OK to operate?' Rob asked, reaching for his ophthalmoscope.

'Don't *you* start,' Ben said. 'Besides, I've got a full list today. Too many public lists get cancelled as it is, without me adding to them. I've got ten patients fasted and all keyed up for their surgery—it's not right to turn them away just because I took a tumble.'

'If you're not up to—'

'I'm fine, for pity's sake,' Ben insisted. 'I've got a bit of gravel rash, that's all. I bet that girl was straight out of med school, brandishing her new skills on whoever she could. Pity she didn't think to brush up on her driving skills while she was at it, especially since she was driving a Porsche.'

'It could have been much worse, Ben,' Rob said with a sober cast to his expression. 'At least she stopped to help you. A lot of people these days would have driven off without a backward glance. Remember that teenage patient three weeks ago? I still have nightmares about telling his parents he didn't make it. It made their ordeal all the harder, having no one stepping up to the plate to take the blame.'

Ben blew out a breath as he finger-combed his hair. 'You're right,' he said. 'I guess that's why this morning rattled me so much. Not only did she stop, this girl was OK to look at, which is some sort of compensation, I suppose.'

Rob's eyes began to twinkle. 'So if you met her again, all would be forgiven?' he asked.

Ben shouldered open the swing doors. 'She was cute but not *that* cute,' he said as he left.

'Where's the new registrar?' Ben asked as he came into Theatre a few minutes later.

'Not here yet,' Linda Reynolds, the scrub nurse, said as she set out the instrument tray.

Ben gave cynical grunt. 'No doubt she's touching up her make-up.'

Linda raised her brows. 'You *are* in a fine mood this morning, Ben. Did you get out of the wrong side of bed or something?'

'Sorry Lindy,' he said gruffly. 'I had a run-in with a car door this morning.'

'That's what you get for cycling to work,' Linda said with a hint of maternal chastisement. 'Why don't you drive a BMW or a Mercedes, like all the other neurosurgeons in Sydney?'

'You sound like my mother,' he said with an easy smile. 'It so happens I wasn't actually cycling to work. I planned to go home and shower and shave and drive back in my ute but I ran out of time.'

The patient was wheeled in and he continued, 'Come on, we'd better get started. I'm not going to wait around for the registrar to turn up.' He looked up at the anaesthetist assigned to his list that morning. 'Things OK your end, Matt?'

'Yes, Ben. I've got all the lines in, and we're ready to induce.'

Ben took the hand of the thirty-five-year-old woman as she was transferred from the trolley to the operating table.

'Hello, Mrs Patonis. You've had a long wait to get into hospital but here you are now. Everything should be fine— we'll resect that meningioma, and hopefully stop those head-aches and improve that weakness,' he reassured her.

'Thanks, Mr Blackwood. I've waited nearly a year to get in,' Maria Patonis said. 'Do you think I'll be able to take up my golf again?'

'Maybe,' he said, touching her arm briefly. 'Let's just stop the damage first, and take things a step at a time. I'll see you after the surgery in Recovery.'

Georgie could feel her stomach churning and twisting with nerves as she ran up the stairs to the operating theatre floor. Turning up late was a no-no in any workplace, but in a busy public hospital, where every minute was so precious, it was not going to win her any favours with the staff. To make things worse, this was her first list on her new term of neuro-surgery. Although from what she'd heard, Ben Blackwood was a very approachable and supportive neurosurgeon, she didn't want to push her luck by getting off to a bad start with him.

She did the preliminary scrub and then gowned and entered the theatre just as the consultant neurosurgeon looked up from the now anaesthetised patient, his dark blue eyes meeting hers.

'Oh my…God,' she gulped, her stomach dropping.

'You must be Georgiana Willoughby,' Linda said, when Ben didn't say a word. 'Welcome to the unit.'

'Er…thank you…' Georgie mumbled. Grimacing, she added weakly, 'Sorry I—I'm late…I had a bit of an accident…'

'How nice that you could make it to join us in spite of your…er…little accident,' Ben said with an unreadable look. 'How about you come over here and draw out where you think the skull flap should be made.'

Georgie bit her lip as she shuffled over. 'I—I can't say I'm totally sure, Mr Blackwood. This is my first neurosurgical term.'

'Yes, I know,' Ben said. 'But the best way to learn is on-the-job experience. So just draw where you think it should go, and we'll correct it if it's a bit off.'

Georgie drew a curved line over the right parietotemporal region of the shaved scalp with a purple marking pen, trying to keep her hands steady under the watchful midnight-blue gaze trained on her.

Wasn't he going to say something? she wondered. Surely he wasn't going to let such an incident pass without a comment or two. As coincidences went, it was up there with the spookiest, which no doubt her flatmate would insist was the celestial forces at work.

Georgie concentrated on the purple line she was drawing and thought about how relieved she was to see he was all right. More than relieved actually. She had been preparing herself for a jail term for negligent driving, although strictly speaking she hadn't been driving so—

'That's pretty good really,' he interrupted her wandering thoughts. 'We just need to make it a bit bigger to make access easier, but the shape and position are fine.'

Georgie felt her shoulders go down in relief. 'Thanks…'

'I'll show you how I like to position, prep and drape for a parietal craniotomy. From then on, I'd like you to set the patient up,' he said.

She watched as he showed her how to position the skull in a head ring and stabilise it in position with braces attached to the sides of the operating table.

Once they had both re-scrubbed and gowned for surgery, Ben showed her how to prep the scalp with Betadine and then drape the skull with adhesive drapes, leaving the operating area exposed.

'Now, if you can make the incision, Dr Willoughby, I'll show you how to control the scalp bleeding with clips. Make the incision down to the periosteum,' he directed.

Georgie made the incision along the pre-marked line, and Ben showed her how to apply stainless-steel clips along the length of the incision to control the bleeding.

'I'll make the first burr-hole,' Ben said as he was handed the air-powered burr, 'and you can do the second, but I'll guide your hand to prevent you from inadvertently pushing too hard.'

Georgie held her breath as his gloved hands came over hers, the strength in his fingers making her stomach and legs go all wobbly. She could smell the warmth of his body, the hint of musky perspiration, not unpleasant but instead disturbingly attractive.

He was not as old as she'd been expecting. It was daft of her really but she was so used to her father's generation of neuro-surgical colleagues that she hadn't factored in the possibility that she would be working alongside a man in his early to mid-thirties. It was hard to tell his exact age but she reasoned he'd have to be at least thirty-four or -five to have completed his training and developed the reputation he had for research.

Georgie also hadn't realised that morning, when he'd been sprawled on the road, how very tall he was. She had vaguely registered his long legs and arms as she had tended to his injuries earlier, but standing so close to him now she could feel his broad chest against her shoulder, which meant he must be more than six feet, possibly three or four inches over, at the very least.

She had, however, noticed his jet-black hair when she'd taken his helmet off and the olive tan of his skin, not to mention the toned muscles of his lean body that suggested he was more than a casual exerciser, which was impressive really when she considered the long hours he worked.

Georgie still couldn't quite believe he hadn't yet referred to their accidental meeting that morning. She had seen some speculative looks coming from the scrub nurse from time to time, but he had remained totally focussed on the patient, his movements steady and controlled, his voice and manner giving no clue as to what had transpired between them a little over an hour ago.

She gave herself a quick mental shake and brought her attention back to the operation where Ben was showing her how to incise the dura without damaging the underlying brain, and within a few minutes the meningioma was exposed.

Removal of the benign tumour seemed very straightforward, although Georgie could see that this was because of Ben's skill and experience, not because the procedure was easy—he just seemed to make it look that way. Within an hour the skull flap had been turned back, the scalp stapled and the head dressed.

* * *

Ben stripped off his gloves and tossed them into the bin as he turned to face the new registrar once the rest of the routine list was over. 'I would like a few words with you in my office.'

She ran the tip of her tongue across her full, shapely lips. 'N-now?' she asked in a squeaky voice.

'Yes, now,' he said with a hint of mockery in his eyes as they held hers. 'Or do you have something else you need to do right this minute?'

She shifted from foot to foot, her creamy cheeks faintly coloured with a rosy hue. 'Um…I was just going to go to the bathroom to…to freshen up…'

Ben had to fight the urge not to roll his eyes. 'Well, once you've touched up your lipstick or whatever it is you're going to do, perhaps you'd care to join me so we can discuss the details of your research project for this year.'

She straightened her shoulders and sent him a toffee-brown glare. 'I'm not wearing lipstick, Mr Blackwood,' she said a little tightly.

Ben felt the corners of his mouth turn up at her little show of defiance. Maybe she had a bit of the old guy in her after all, he thought, although she certainly didn't look anything like him. Her slender frame was athletic but utterly feminine, her lightly tanned skin smooth and her light brown hair with its natural-looking golden highlights a perfect foil for those big brown Bambi-like eyes of hers. Her mouth was pulled a little tight right now, but earlier he'd noticed the soft plumpness of her lips when her small white but perfect teeth had sunk into them.

Yep, she was cute all right but she damned well could have killed him and he wasn't going to let her off that easily.

'Right, then,' he said as he moved past, 'I'll be waiting for you in my office.'

* * *

'Don't worry about Mr Blackwood,' Linda said to Georgie in the theatre change room a short time later. 'He's had a bit of a rough start to the day. He's normally very affable. He's everyone's favourite. There's actually a staff waiting list to work in his theatre. That's very unusual for a neurosurgical theatre, I can tell you.' She bundled her theatre scrubs and tossed them in the laundry bin as she went on, 'Apparently some crazy woman knocked him off his bike this morning. It was a miracle he wasn't badly injured.'

Georgie swallowed and concentrated fiercely on washing her hands. 'That's…er…awful,' she said.

'I've been warning him for years about cycling on city streets,' Linda said as she stretched her lips to apply lipstick. She recapped the tube and added, 'We had a hit-and-run death a few weeks back. The paramedics did all they could to save him but he died in A and E from his head injuries. One of the nurses went on stress leave as a result. Her son was the same age.'

Georgie ran her tongue over her dry-as-dust lips. 'Mr Blackwood's…er…accident wasn't a hit and run, though, was it?'

'No, thank God,' Linda said, and, picking up her bag, gave Georgie a friendly smile. 'Ben's a real softie. And you wear all the lipstick you like, my girl. What that boy needs is to take his mind off work for a change. A hospital romance is just what this place needs to liven things up a bit.'

Georgie tossed her head as she turned from the basin. 'I'm not interested in anything but my career,' she said. 'Anyway, I've taken a temporary no-dating pact with my flatmate Rhiannon. If either of us breaks, we have to pay the other a thousand dollars.'

Linda pushed open the door. 'Then you'd better start saving, Dr Willoughby,' she said with a gleaming smile. 'I don't like your chances.'

Georgie turned to look at her reflection in the mirror once the scrub nurse had left. 'We'll see about that,' she said, and, giving her head another toss, walked out to where she had seen Mr Blackwood's name on a door down the corridor.

The door was ajar but she knocked anyway and waited for his command to come in.

'You can close the door after you,' he said as she entered the small office.

Georgie closed the door with a little click and walked the short distance to his desk where he was sitting with some papers in front of him. She noticed his dark blue gaze dip to her mouth and her resentment rose like a flash flood inside her. So he thought she was an empty-headed bimbo who had nothing better to do that paint her mouth with lipstick, did he?

'So,' he drawled, leaning back in his chair in an indolent manner. 'Who taught you to drive? Your mother or your father?'

Georgie drew herself up to her full height, which wasn't all that impressive without her heels, her mouth tight with barely controlled anger. 'I know it was technically my fault but you were riding far too close to the row of parked cars,' she said. 'There was no need to be that close. If it hadn't been me opening my door on you, it could just have easily been someone else.'

A flare of something diamond-hard lit his gaze as it collided with hers. 'But it *was* you, Dr Willoughby,' he said. 'And as a *doctor*—not to mention a *neurosurgical registrar*— you should know the dangers of such reckless disregard for other road users.'

'I wasn't disregarding anyone,' Georgie shot back quickly, annoyed at the way he seemed to be over-emphasising her responsibility as a trained medico. 'I accidentally left my mobile phone in the gym so I pulled over and opened my door without thinking.'

His expression was full of cynicism as he held her defensive look. 'You. Didn't. Think,' he said with a sardonic curl of his top lip. 'That's not exactly a quality I want in a registrar, Dr Willoughby. I would have thought someone from your distinctive medical family would have picked up that skill along the way.'

Georgie tightened her hands into fists by her sides. 'I came here to apologise but I can see now it's going to be pointless,' she bit out. 'You're obviously going to make me pay by giving me a bad report at the end of my term with you. That's totally unfair. I should be treated just like anyone else, in spite of what happened this morning.'

He got to his feet, the sound of his chair rolling along the floor shattering the stiff silence. 'You could have killed me,' he said through taut lips. 'I could be lying under a sheet with a tag on my toe in the morgue right now because you didn't think. Have you *thought* about that, Dr Willoughby?'

Georgie had and it had churned her stomach all morning, but something about his overbearing attitude made her reluctant to admit it. 'You're blowing this all out of proportion,' she said. 'You weren't even injured.'

'Which shows how unobservant you were at the time,' he returned. 'You were too keen to show off your roadside retrieval skills, weren't you, Dr Willoughby?'

She straightened her spine even further. 'I did what any EMST-trained medico would have done.'

His top lip curled again. 'You have a lot to learn. And unfortunately I am the one who is assigned to teach you. I hope you know what you're letting yourself in for.'

She sent him a sharp glare. 'I can handle whatever you dish out, Mr Blackwood,' she said. 'My father warned me about men like you.'

'Did he now?' Ben asked with a slant of one dark brow.

'Yes,' she said, putting up her chin. 'You've obviously got a chip on your shoulder about my background but I've worked damned hard to earn a place on the training scheme and I'm not going to let someone like you sabotage my career.'

'I don't give a flying fig about your background but I do care about the standard of care my patients are exposed to,' he clipped out. 'If you put one foot wrong I'm going to have to pull you into line. Do you understand?'

'Perfectly,' she said, her brown eyes flashing with fury. 'Will that be all, Mr Blackwood?'

Don't look at her mouth, Ben told himself sternly as he gripped the edge of his desk, his groin tightening in spite of everything he tried to do to stop it. He could feel the crackling energy of her body coming towards him, his nostrils flaring as the flowery fragrance of her perfume drifted his way.

'Yes,' he said. 'That is all—for now. We'll talk about your research project later.'

He watched as she spun around and stalked out with her head held high, her neat little bottom outlined by the scrubs she was still wearing, the legs far too long for her with her feet still in theatre clogs.

Uh-oh. He inwardly winced as the door shut abruptly behind her.

He raked a hand through his hair and blew out a whooshing breath as he listened to her stomping footsteps fade into the distance.

Double uh-oh.

CHAPTER THREE

'So how was your first day?' Rhiannon asked as Georgie came home later that evening.

Georgie tossed her bag on the sofa and clamped her hands to the sides of her head above her ears. *'Arrrggghhhh!'*

Rhiannon winced. 'Oh, dear,' she said. 'That doesn't sound so good.'

'I cannot believe everyone thinks that man is God's gift to the public health system,' Georgie ranted. 'He was insufferable!'

'Insufferable, huh?' Rhiannon curled up on the sofa and, tucking a cushion against her middle, waited patiently to hear the rest.

'Yes,' Georgie said, still pacing the floor in agitation. 'Insufferable, arrogant, rude and…and…'

'Nice-looking?' Rhiannon offered helpfully.

Georgie turned to face her with an irritated expression on her face. 'That's completely irrelevant.'

Rhiannon's finely arched brows lifted. 'Is it?'

'Of course it is,' Georgie said. 'You know what we said. No dating until after Easter.'

'Just checking,' Rhiannon said with a little grin. 'So what did he do to get you so hot under the collar?'

'Well…' Georgie nibbled at her lip for a moment. 'I guess it was *sort of* my fault…' she said, and gave her friend a quick overview of the morning's events.

When she had finished Rhiannon gave her a wide-eyed look. 'That's really spooky,' she said. Tapping her chin thoughtfully, she added, 'I wonder what Madame Celestia would make of that.'

Georgie rolled her eyes. 'Madame Celestia is a fraudulent charlatan,' she said. 'Besides, how come she had to cancel your last appointment due to unforeseen circumstances? And if she's such a great fortune-teller why does she need an appointment book anyway? She should know exactly who's coming and when.'

Rhiannon tossed the cushion to one side as she got to her feet. 'I know you're a sceptic but don't forget she predicted my sister's pregnancy *and* she predicted it was going to be a girl before Caitlin had even had an ultrasound.'

'She had a fifty-fifty chance of being right, for heaven's sake,' Georgie pointed out. 'Anyway, Caitlin probably gave off a thousand clues the first time she went. It's called cold-reading, Rhiannon.'

'Madame Celestia told me you were going to marry a doctor,' Rhiannon said authoritatively. 'And she said he was blond.'

'What?' Georgie stared at her. 'You mean you consulted her about *me*?'

Rhiannon gave a little offhand shrug. 'I didn't see any harm in it, especially as you don't even believe in any of it anyway.'

'But that's not the point,' Georgie protested. 'I don't like the thought of someone speculating about me. It doesn't seem right. I want to forge my own destiny, not have it thrust on me by the power of suggestion.'

Rhiannon folded her arms. 'What colour hair does Mr Blackwood have?'

'Oh, for pity's sake!' Georgie said. 'You surely don't for a moment think I would be interested in that…that arrogant, stuck-up, I'm-your-boss-and-you-will-do-what-I-say jerk, do you?'

Rhiannon tilted her head. 'What colour?'

'Black as the ace of spades,' Georgie informed her. 'And not a grey hair in sight, in case Madame Celestia got her wires crossed.'

'Oh, well, that's settled, then,' Rhiannon said. 'He's not the one for you.'

Georgie rolled her eyes again. 'Thank God.'

The supermarket was crowded at that time of the evening, professional people rushing in on their way home, all jostling to get last-minute items for dinner. Georgie wandered up and down the aisles with her basket as she waited for the queues to ease down a bit.

Shopping for herself was still a bit of a novelty for her, having only just moved away from home. She knew twenty-seven was rather old to be leaving the nest but she'd been perfectly happy living with her parents up until her father had retired a few weeks before Christmas. Ever since then both he and her mother had started to butt in on her life, as if theirs had come to a sudden end. Georgie recognised the very great adjustment her father had yet to make in moving from a demanding and stressful surgical and teaching career to being a retiree with no pressing commitments other than a few casual rounds of golf. Many retiring medical specialists suffered the same doubts and insecurities once their career identity was removed. And she also recognised the changes her mother was undergoing in having twenty-four hours a day, seven days a week access to a husband she had rarely seen in the past thirty years of their marriage.

Her father's generous offer to buy an apartment for her had precipitated Georgie into deciding it was time to move out and leave them to it. Besides, she had to study, and study hard, to get through four years of neurosurgical training. Although after today's ignominious beginning she was starting to suffer doubts and insecurities of her own.

She looked up to check the condition of the queues and locked gazes with a midnight-blue one. Her mouth went dry and her heart started to thump, her hand on the basket handle moistening.

She turned away and feigned an avid interest in the confectionary display in front of her, hoping he would just ignore her and move on.

'Good evening, Dr Willoughby.'

No such luck, Georgie thought sourly as she slowly turned around to face him. 'Good evening, Mr Blackwood,' she said in a distinctly cool tone.

Ben's eyes went to the basket she was carrying. His mother always said you could tell a lot about a person from how they shopped. Fresh fruit, low-fat yoghurt, wholegrain bread and…two chocolate bars. Somehow that made him smile inwardly. His younger sister Hannah was exactly the same— perhaps it was a girl thing.

He had been feeling a little bit guilty about reading the Riot Act to Georgie the way he had. She was young and inexperienced but clearly eager to learn, and the accident after all had been exactly that: an accident. She had probably been nervous and preoccupied on her first day, which every registrar, including himself, had experienced.

His eyes did a quick scan of her stiff little figure, standing with her basket like a shield against her, those big brown eyes of hers unwavering as they held his, and he felt his groin tighten another notch.

Yep, she was cute all right.

'Doing your shopping?' he asked, in an attempt to ease the tense atmosphere.

'Yes,' she said with a little lift of her chin. 'You?'

He indicated the basket in his hand and gave her a rueful smile in spite of the hostile glare she was sending his way. 'Yes. I always seem to be missing the most important ingredient when I start to cook.'

She made to move past. 'I'd better not keep you, then.'

'It's all right,' he said, touching her on the arm. He saw her flinch and dropped his hand from the satin softness of her bare skin, his fingers still tingling from the contact. Her brown eyes were still fixed on his, unblinking.

'Do you live around here?' he asked into the tight silence.

'Yes.'

'Where exactly?'

'Beachside Apartments, on the promenade,' she answered.

No doubt Daddy's bought his little girl a penthouse, Ben thought cynically. The real estate on that Bondi Beach block was phenomenally expensive. He'd bought three streets back and was still wondering how he was going to pay it off before he retired.

'Look, Georgina—' he began.

'Georgiana,' she said with cutting emphasis.

'Oh, well, then,' he said, deliberately dragging out the syllables, 'Geor-gi-a-na.'

She lifted her chin even higher, her toffee-brown eyes sending off sparks. 'But I prefer Georgie.'

'Georgiè.' He tasted her name on his lips, wondering how his would sound on hers. He put out his free hand, his eyes still holding hers. 'I'm Ben, by the way.'

She ignored his hand. 'Excuse me,' she said. 'I have someone waiting for me.'

Ben let his hand fall back to his side as she strode over to the checkouts, her back rigid with haughtiness. She didn't even look his way when she'd paid for her items. She simply gave the checkout attendant an on-off smile, picked up her bag and left.

Ben rolled his lips together, a tiny kernel of anger hardening inside him at her stuck-up rudeness as he snatched up three chocolate bars and moved towards the checkouts.

'So how's your new registrar working out?' Madeleine Brothers, Associate Professor of Neurosurgery, asked in the doctors' room the next morning. 'I heard she ran you down yesterday.'

Ben stopped stirring his coffee to look at her. 'Amazing how much the story gets changed during transmission,' he remarked wryly. 'She didn't run me down—she opened her car door on me.'

'Are you all right?'

'Of course I'm all right.'

'If you want to swap her to our unit, that could be organised,' Madeleine offered.

Ben frowned as he examined the contents of his cup. 'No, that won't be necessary, I'm sure we'll get along fine after she's settled in a little.'

'I heard she's very beautiful,' Madeleine commented in a laid-back, mildly interested tone.

His head came up at that. 'I hadn't noticed.'

One of Madeleine's brows rose. 'Even the comatose patients have noticed it, Ben,' she responded dryly. 'But you know my rules on fraternising with junior staff.'

Ben sat up straighter in his chair, his frown taking on a brooding edge. 'Come on, Madeleine, there's no law against it. This isn't senior high school. We're all mature adults.'

She folded her arms and gave him a contemplative look. 'So you have noticed her, huh?'

'Yes, but don't worry. I'm not interested.' *Liar! Of course you're interested—what man wouldn't be?* He scowled darkly and added, 'She's got the same imperious everyone-is-beneath-me air as her father.'

'Yes, well, I reckon Bevis Willoughby would be the father-in-law from hell,' Madeleine said with grimace. 'No one, and I mean *no one,* is going to be good enough for his precious princess.'

Ben rolled his eyes as he got to his feet. 'Tell me about it,' he said. 'I pity the guy who gets the job of asking for his daughter's hand in marriage.'

Madeleine lifted her brows again. 'Do men still do that these days?' she asked, reaching for the coffee-pot.

'My late father did,' Ben said. 'And even my stepfather asked for a private meeting with my grandfather. I guess eventually I'll have to follow their example.'

'So in spite of public opinion, country-bred men are much more sophisticated and refined than they are given credit for,' Madeleine mused.

'Try telling that to Professor Willoughby,' Ben said as he shouldered open the door. 'He used to glance at my shoes during every Monday morning tutorial to check for cow manure.'

Madeleine laughed. 'Did you bring some in to annoy him?'

Ben grinned. 'What do you think?' he said, and, winking at her, left.

The accident happened right in front of her. Georgie slammed on the brakes as the car in front of her ran into the one in front of it, the sound of metal crunching against metal sickening to say the least.

She pulled slightly towards the centre of the road to prevent more cars from ramming up the back of the already crashed vehicles, and turned on her hazard lights. There had been a case recently of a good Samaritan rescue gone wrong when another car had severely injured a rescuer. She'd resolved in a similar situation to put her car between herself and any rescue mission she undertook. She approached the car in front where a woman in her early thirties was looking pale and upset, her small infant crying volubly in the babyseat in the back.

An older man was getting out of the first car, his face puce with anger as he strode over to the young mother. 'What the hell you do think you're doing, you stupid idiot?' he stormed. 'Didn't you see the red light or are you just plain dumb?'

'Excuse me, sir,' Georgie said, as she placed her doctor's bag on the road. 'I'm a doctor. Are you hurt in any way?'

The man peered down at her. 'No, but I want to press charges for—'

'Never mind that now,' Georgie interrupted firmly. 'Step back and out of the way. I need to see to this young woman's baby. You can sort your grievances out later. Go and wait by your car until the police arrive.'

The man looked as if he was going to argue the point but Georgie had already opened her bag and slung her stethoscope around her neck to drive home her professional advantage.

She turned to the mother and smiled reassuringly. 'Don't worry, he'll soon cool down. Now, let's have a look at you both.'

'I'm fine,' the young mother said, wiping away tears of distress. 'But Jasmine…'

'Is that your name, sweetie?' Georgie crooned as she expertly examined the baby girl, who looked about eight months old. 'Did you get a big nasty shock when Mummy's car suddenly stopped?'

'Is she all right?' the mother asked with a wobble in her voice.

'I can't see anything wrong with her,' Georgie said as she did a hasty primary survey up to ABCD, missing out on E. As she listened to the little girl's chest with her stethoscope, she wasn't sure whether she'd heard a faint murmur. When she listened again she couldn't definitely pick it up. She pulled the baby's top back down and tickled her under the chin before addressing the mother.

'It seems like all is OK,' Georgie said, 'but she needs to be checked over properly at Accident and Emergency just to make sure everything is fine. I've already called an ambulance. It's possible the restraints on her baby seat may have bruised her when the car stopped.'

'I didn't see the man's brake lights,' the young mother began to cry again.

'Try not to upset yourself,' Georgie said, putting a consoling hand on the woman's shoulder. 'Jasmine is probably crying because you are, aren't you, poppet?'

The little baby gave her a toothless smile, two fat crystal tears still clinging to her blonde eyelashes, but thankfully her wailing had stopped.

Within a few moments a police car arrived, closely followed by the ambulance, the paramedics agreeing with Georgie's advice to transport the baby to A and E for assessment. While the paramedics extracted the child from her seat with neck support, and onto a trolley, Georgie wrote basic notes and obs onto a paper pad from her car, and gave it to the ambulance driver to add to their own hospital notes.

After the ambulance had left, Georgie stopped to have a quick chat with the policewoman attending the accident. She knew her from the gym and had often exchanged an early-morning greeting with her in the change room in the past. 'Hi, Belinda,' she said. 'Fancy meeting you here.'

Belinda Bronson smiled. 'I didn't see you at the fit ball class this morning.'

'I was on call last night and slept through my alarm.'

Belinda ran her gaze over Georgie's neat skirt and top and mid-height heels. 'You know, I almost didn't recognise you with your clothes on.'

Georgie grinned. 'No wonder they've banned camera phones in the gym.'

'You'd be amazed at what people get up to,' Belinda said, with a fleeting but totally cynical cop-like expression. 'You off to work now?'

Georgie glanced at her watch and grimaced. *'Hell!* I'm going to be late for my first ward round on the neurosurgical unit.'

'Thanks for helping here this morning,' Belinda said. 'That little baby was a cutie, wasn't she?'

'Don't tell me you're a bit clucky.'

'I'm over thirty now so, yes, I'm hearing the clock tick a little louder than before.'

Georgie smiled at her friend's rueful expression. 'You doing body combat tomorrow morning?'

Belinda gave her a twinkling look as she pointed to the tall, good-looking police officer who was inspecting the brake lights of the male driver's car. 'I'm hoping to be doing body combat *tonight*. What do you think of my new partner?'

Georgie ran her gaze over the fit-looking, brown-haired man. 'Not bad,' she said.

'What about you? Got any options going at that new hospital of yours?' Belinda asked.

Georgie had to forcibly remove the image of Ben Blackwood from her mind. 'I'm on a three-month no-dating pact,' she said. 'My flatmate and I decided after our last relationship disasters we were going to bail out for a while. I'm *so* over men at the moment.'

'No wonder you're hitting the gym every morning,' Belinda said, reaching for her phone when it started to buzz. 'Catch you later, Georgie.'

'See you,' Georgie answered. Glancing at her watch again she raced back to her car.

CHAPTER FOUR

'SO WHERE is the registrar this morning?' Ben asked Irene Clark, the unit head nurse on duty.

'She called the unit a few minutes ago. She's going to be a few minutes late,' Irene said. 'She said something about an accident.'

Ben gave a grunt and turned to the four medical students and the intern hovering in the background. 'Just for the record if you need to make up an excuse for being absent or late, make sure it's an original each time,' he said. 'I will be keeping a mental record of how many grandmothers' funerals, toothaches or minor traffic accidents occur.'

There was a snigger from the group just as Georgie burst onto the ward. 'Sorry I'm so late,' she said a little breathlessly. 'I was caught up in an accident and—'

Ben hooked one brow upwards. 'Another one, Dr Willoughby?'

Georgie stopped in her tracks, her eyes taking in the interested stares from the medical students and Jules Littlemore the intern. She drew her shoulders back and met Ben's dark satirical gaze with an equanimity fuelled by anger. 'Yes, as a matter of fact, Mr Blackwood,' she said in a clipped tone. 'And this time it wasn't my fault.'

The corner of his mouth lifted in a smirk. 'I'm very glad to hear it. Now, if you'd like to join us, we're about to do a ward round. You do know what that is, don't you Dr Willoughby?'

Georgie silently seethed as he led the way to the first patient. So that's the way he was going to play it, was he? She ground her teeth as she took her place beside Jeffrey Neale's bed.

'Dr Willoughby, can you summarise Mr Neale's admission from last night for us, please?' Ben asked as he glanced through the patient's notes. 'Mr DeBurgh has asked me to include his patients on the ward round for him as he's doing a list in the private hospital this morning.'

'Yes, Mr Blackwood,' Georgie answered tightly. 'Mr Neale came in through A and E after a high-speed MVA. He was resussed and investigated by the A and E staff before I was called. Apart from some minor soft-tissue injuries and a couple of fractured ribs, his main problem was a closed head injury, and his GCS was 9 on arrival. He was intubated and CT'd. He's got diffuse oedema and scattered cerebral petechial haemorrhages but no localising lesion. Last night Mr DeBurgh put in an ICP monitor. He's been on mannitol, steroids and phenobarb overnight. ICP has remained normal, and pCO_2 and oximetry have been closely monitored.'

'Nicely summarised, Georgie,' Jules said with an encouraging smile.

'Yes, not bad,' Ben agreed. 'But you haven't gone on to the management plan.'

Georgie set her mouth. 'I thought you just wanted the summary up to now.'

Ben held her pointed look. 'The summary is fine. But you need to spell out a plan of management. You can't just stop there.'

Her eyes shifted away from his. 'Sorry,' she mumbled.

Ben could tell she wasn't the least bit sorry. She had a pout on her mouth and her chin was a little too high for his liking.

He forced his attention back to the matter in hand and said, 'Maybe the students can help us out, then. Karen, what do you think we should be doing with Mr Neale today?

'Well, I think we should maybe re-CT him to make sure no focal bleed has occurred, because we can't do a clinical neurological assessment. Then maybe start to withdraw the sedation and see what sort of GCS and peripheral neuro activity we get,' Karen answered. 'Oh, and maybe an EEG, too.'

'That's not bad for a medical student,' Ben said. 'Karen, why don't you work with Dr Willoughby and write down a management plan, and we'll review it later this morning?'

'Gee, thanks, Mr Blackwood. I'd be glad to help out,' Karen gushed.

Georgie caught Jules's amused gaze and rolled her eyes.

The next patient was a woman in her early fifties who had undergone a microdiscectomy a few days previously. Georgie gave the students a quick rundown on Mrs Walters's progress before addressing the patient. 'So how is the physiotherapy going, Mrs Walters?'

'I'm not very good on the stairs yet,' Margaret Walters confessed. 'And the pain is keeping me awake at night.'

'It takes time for things to settle down,' Ben said, his shoulder brushing Georgie's as he reached past her to inspect the IV fluid chart. 'We'll write up some more pain relief for you but I'd like to see you walking down the corridor tomorrow. I don't expect you to do a marathon but it's important to get moving. And don't forget—no sitting for two weeks and no lifting or bending for six.'

'I don't know how I'll manage,' Margaret said with a worried frown. 'My husband's not well and we've got our disabled son to care for. Who's going to do the washing and cooking?'

Ben put the chart back, noticing how Georgie had put some distance between them. 'I'll send one of the social workers in to chat to you about home help,' he said. 'And perhaps you'd better have a few extra days in hospital to give yourself a bit more of a break.'

Georgie fell back as the ward round came to an end to chat with Jules, who had attended the same university as herself and Rhiannon. He had briefly dated a friend of hers and while he and Emma had since broken up, Georgie and Rhiannon had maintained occasional contact with him.

'So what's going on with you and Ben Blackwood?' Jules asked with a teasing smile. 'I've never seen him act like that before. He's normally so laid back and easygoing.'

Georgie checked to see if anyone could hear them before answering with a scowl, 'I disliked him the moment I met him. He's a pain in the you-know-where.'

'Uh-oh,' Jules said.

'What do you mean, "Uh-oh"?' Georgie asked, frowning at him darkly.

He gave her another grin. 'You don't stand a chance, Georgie,' he said. 'Pay Rhiannon the thousand bucks and get it over with.'

She gave him a surprised glance. 'She told you about that?'

'Yeah,' he said, not quite meeting her eyes. 'I ran into her the other night.'

'Funny she didn't mention anything to me,' Georgie said with a smile and a glint in her eye.

'Dr Willoughby.' Ben Blackwood's voice cut through the air like a switchblade. 'If you have finished flirting with the intern, I would like to see you in my office to discuss your research project.'

Georgie turned around but he was already striding away.

She turned back to Jules and said in an undertone, 'See what I mean? A total pain in the rear end.'

Jules just smiled.

This time his office door was closed and Georgie stood outside it for a moment, trying to control her bubbling anger. She took a couple of calming breaths and clenched and un-clenched her fists.

'Are you to going to knock on it or kick it in?' Ben asked from just behind her.

She spun around, her colour rising as she met his mocking eyes. 'I suppose you think it's hilariously funny, making a laughing stock of me in front of the medical students, do you?' she said.

He reached past her to open the door, his arm brushing against her waist. Georgie stepped away but her body felt hot and tingly and her nostrils began to flare as the tantalising scent of his aftershave drifted towards her. She fought against her reaction and not just for the sake of a thousand dollars. He was quite clearly enjoying every moment of her discom-fiture if the look in his bluer-than-blue gaze was to be believed.

'Would you like a coffee or something?' he asked as he took the chair behind his desk.

'No, thank you,' she said, still standing.

'Would you like to sit down or are you enjoying the height advantage for a change?'

'You really are the most annoying man I've ever met,' she bit out. 'You've done nothing but ridicule me from the word go. Just where do you get off?'

A hint of steel entered his voice. 'Sit down, Dr Willoughby.'

She stamped her foot on the floor. 'No, I will not sit down.'

A flash of anger appeared in his eyes as they duelled with hers. 'Do you want to stay on this unit or not, Dr Willoughby?'

Her eyes burned into his. 'Are you threatening me, Mr Blackwood?'

He got to his feet in one slow movement, his increase in height making her feel tiny as he towered over her with only the desk between them. Her stomach did a funny little bird-like flutter as he leant forward with his hands resting on the desk, his eyes pinning hers.

'You have been late two mornings in a row,' he said in a cold, hard tone. 'I do not usually like to run the unit like a drill sergeant but if you keep not turning up on time we'll have to look at whether you're suitable for the neurosurgical training scheme.'

'If you do that I will report you to the CEO. My father and he are golf buddies.' As soon as Georgie had said the words she regretted them. She was not normally a name-dropper and she positively loathed hospital politics, but something about Ben's manner towards her provoked her into totally uncharacteristic behaviour.

His eyes glittered like sapphires, his jaw white with anger. 'You really take the cake, don't you, Dr Willoughby?' he said. 'You come flouncing into my unit like a princess, expecting everyone to worship the very ground you walk on just because you happen to have a professor for a father.'

'I do *not* flounce,' she said, only just managing to resist a toss of her head.

His lip curled. 'I'm not impressed with anything I've seen from you so far,' he said. 'You came to that ward round unprepared and then had the audacity to flirt with the intern.'

'The intern and I are friends,' she said in her defence, her cheeks glowing with rage. 'And I do *not* flirt.'

'Is there anything else you do *not* do?' he asked with another curl of his lip.

Georgie had had enough. She leaned forward on the desk, the tips of her splayed fingers touching his, her eyes like twin fires as she met him eye to eye. 'I do not normally feel like slapping my boss's face but let me tell you right now I am sorely tempted.'

'Go right ahead,' he said, eyeballing her back. 'But perhaps I should warn you of the consequences first.'

Georgie disguised a little swallow as her gaze dipped to his mouth. She was so close to him she could see the pepper of dark stubble on his face as if he had skipped shaving that morning. It gave him an arrantly masculine look that was devastatingly attractive. She tried to edge her fingers away from his but somehow one of his hands had come down over both of hers, trapping them beneath his.

'W-what consequences?' she croaked as her eyes returned to his.

Long seconds seemed to pass before he spoke.

'I'm not going to tolerate this sort of performance, Dr Willoughby. If there is any more slacking off, you'll be out on your ear. Understood?'

'Perfectly,' she said through tight lips.

He released her hands as he straightened, his hands going to his trouser pockets, the deep thrust of them drawing her eyes like a magnet. He had such long, strong legs, toned by hours of hard exercise, his waist lean and his stomach flat and ridged with muscle that was clearly visible through the lightweight cotton of his shirt. His sleeves were rolled back past his wrists, the dark masculine hair reminding her all over again of his potency as a full-blooded male in his prime.

She brought her gaze back to his, her colour rising again at the hint of mockery still lurking in his expression.

'Everything to your liking, Dr Willoughby?' he asked. 'Or are you just checking to see if I need another bandage or two?'

She sent him a fulminating glare without answering but she could feel the heat of her embarrassment crawling like flames all over her face.

'So who was the lucky recipient of your expert roadside help this morning?' he asked with another taunting smile. 'Or did you just make that up to get a few extra minutes in your boyfriend's bed?'

Georgie clenched her hands by her sides. 'I do *not* have a boyfriend and the person I attended to was brought into A and E by ambulance. For your information, I'm going down there right now to check on her progress.'

Ben suppressed a frown as she swung away, her high ponytail swishing from side to side as she wrenched open the door and left.

He removed his hands from his trouser pockets and dragged one through his hair as he sat back down at his desk and began mentally rehearsing his apology.

'How did things go with little Jasmine?' Georgie asked Jennifer Patterson, the doctor on duty in A and E.

'She was fine in terms of the accident,' Jennifer answered. 'But you did the right thing sending her in about that suspected heart murmur. I don't know why it wasn't picked up earlier. We've organised an appointment with Cardiology for an echo.'

'Gosh,' Georgie said on an expelled breath. 'That was lucky. I guess some accidents are meant to happen.'

Jennifer's green eyes began to twinkle. 'Everyone's talking about your little accident yesterday with Ben Blackwood,' she said. 'That was a spooky coincidence, wasn't it?'

Georgie started to scowl. 'Who told you about it? I was under the impression Mr Blackwood wasn't going to mention it but apparently he has, no doubt to rub salt in the wound.'

'Actually, I heard it from one of the paramedics,' Jennifer said. 'He recognised you from your term at RPA.'

'Oh…'

'So has Ben forgiven you yet?' Jennifer asked.

'No, and I don't think he's going to,' she said with a worried frown. 'He's threatening to pull me out of the training scheme.'

Jennifer's neat brows lifted. 'That doesn't sound like Ben,' she said. 'Mind you, with what happened to his sister, I guess he would be feeling a bit touchy.'

'What happened to his sister?'

'She was knocked off her bike when she was seven years old,' she said. 'Hit and run from what I've heard.'

'Was she…?' Georgie gulped over the word. 'Killed?'

Jennifer shook her head. 'No, but she suffered quite serious head injuries. She's OK now, or so I've been told. Ben doesn't talk about it and we know better than to ask. We had another hit and run in here just recently. The poor lad didn't make it so I guess it would have been on Ben's mind when you tipped him off his bike.'

'Oh, my God,' Georgie said, her chest feeling prickly and tight. 'I feel so awful…'

'It can happen to anyone,' Jennifer said. 'This place is full of people who get struck down by the hand of fate. It's called life.'

'I'll have to apologise,' Georgie said, biting her lip.

'You mean you haven't already?'

'I did, but he didn't listen,' she answered, fighting back another scowl.

Jennifer gave her a musing look. 'Uh-oh,' she said.

Georgie's scowl turned into a frown. 'Is that some sort of secret Sydney Metropolitan language?' she asked. 'Jules Littlemore said the very same thing a short time ago.'

Jennifer just smiled.

* * *

Georgie was on her way back to Ben's office when she was paged by Richard DeBurgh, one of the other neurosurgeons. She had covered his on-call the night before and had been looking forward to meeting him after his positive comments on how she had handled things during the night.

She knocked on his office door and entered at his command to come in.

'Ah, Georgie, come in and make yourself comfortable,' Richard said. 'How is your father enjoying his retirement?'

Georgie took the chair opposite and sent him a friendly smile. 'He's finding it a bit difficult adjusting to a quieter pace,' she confessed. 'But he's lost some weight since Christmas, which is a good thing.'

'We miss him here,' he said. 'His work for the research foundation was brilliant. Is he continuing his role as chief patron?'

'I'm not sure,' Georgie said. 'I think my mother is hoping he will put himself back on some committees or boards. He's starting to get under her feet.'

Richard chuckled. 'My wife has already warned me to ease into retirement gradually rather than come to a complete stop. So how have your first two days been?'

Her face fell a little. 'OK, I guess…'

'Come on, tell me what's happened, my dear,' he said. 'Have you had some trouble?'

Georgie decided it wouldn't hurt to get an ally on board, especially a senior clinician. 'Ben Blackwood and I got off to a very bad start,' she said. 'I'm not sure if I'm going to be able to put things right between us.'

'It's probably more to do with your father than you, Georgie,' he said in response. 'I suppose you know Ben failed his fellowship first time around.'

She felt a frown tug at her forehead. 'No…I didn't know that.'

'Your father was the examiner who failed him.'

The pennies were starting to drop rather loudly in Georgie's head. 'Oh… I didn't know that either.'

'Petty of him, if you ask me,' Richard said. 'Ben, I mean, not your father, of course,' he added with a little smile. 'Just do your best, my dear, and I'll make sure my report on you more than makes up for anything Ben Blackwood might say against you.'

'Thank you, Mr DeBurgh. That's very kind of you.'

'Please, call me Richard,' he said as he got to his feet. 'Unlike some others around here, I don't stand on ceremony.' He offered her his hand across the desk. 'Welcome to the unit, Georgie. It's a pleasure to have you on board.'

Georgie smiled as she shook his hand. 'Thank you, Richard. I'm looking forward to working with you.'

CHAPTER FIVE

'HAS anyone seen Dr Willoughby about?' Ben asked in the unit later that day.

'I think she's left for the day,' the afternoon shift nurse Carla Yates informed him. 'She was on call last night so I expect she was feeling a bit tired. It was a busy night. Do you want me to get her on the line for you?'

'No,' he said, reaching for his phone. 'I'll call her myself. It's not urgent.'

'She's nothing like her father, is she?' Carla asked after a little pause.

Ben looked at her with as little animation as possible. 'What?'

'Georgie Willoughby,' she said. 'She's rather a sweetie, don't you think?'

He gave the nurse a noncommittal shrug. 'She's OK, I guess.'

'Jennifer Patterson was telling me Georgie quite possibly saved a young baby's life this morning,' she carried on.

Ben felt another wave of remorse begin to tighten his stomach. 'Oh, really?'

'Yes, she was first on the scene at a minor accident but insisted on the baby being brought in for observation. It turns out the little girl had an undiagnosed cardiac murmur. She was echoed this afternoon and has mitral incompetence.'

'That was a lucky pick-up,' he said, mentally escalating his apology.

'Sure was.'

'Well, then,' he said giving the nurse a quick smile, 'I'll be off.'

'Doing anything special this evening, Ben?' she asked.

'Not really. A quick session in the gym and then dinner and bed.'

'Sounds a bit boring to me,' Carla said. 'Isn't it time you put Leila behind you and went on a date?'

'My lack of dating recently has nothing whatsoever to do with my break-up with Leila,' he said with a brooding frown. 'I just haven't had the time.'

Carla patted his arm as she moved to answer the ringing phone. 'You should make the time.'

I might just do that, Ben thought as he pressed the button for the lift.

Georgie hated going to the gym in the evenings. She was a morning person and liked the feeling of having put her exercise behind her for the day so she could concentrate on work and study. But being on call two nights a week and every third weekend was going to disrupt her routine and she decided she'd better try and be a bit more flexible.

She didn't recognise any of the faces in the cardio room, which meant no chatting to the person beside her on the step machine or cross-trainer.

She was half way through her warm-up when she saw Ben come in. He was dressed in a dry-skin workout top and bicycle shorts, every muscle pumped and glowing from lifting weights in the next room.

She put her head down and upped the speed on the cross-trainer, hoping he wouldn't recognise her.

She felt him rather than saw him. Every tiny hair on the back of her neck lifted when she picked up that totally intoxicating intermingled scent of his body and aftershave.

'Hi,' he said, taking the treadmill machine beside her.

'Oh…hi…' She blinked the perspiration out of her eyes and brushed her hair back with her hand.

'I haven't seen you in here before,' he said as he selected a programme.

Georgie concentrated on the calorie readout rather than meet his eyes. *What? Only forty-eight? An apple was at least eighty!* 'I usually come in the mornings,' she said. 'But I overslept this morning.'

'But not because of a boyfriend.'

She swivelled her head his way. 'Er…no…'

'I've never actually apologised on a treadmill before so, please, excuse me if it's a little rough around the edges,' he said. 'I was out of line this morning.'

Georgie turned back to concentrate on her heart rate readout this time. *One hundred and eighty! Surely that couldn't be right?* 'It's fine, really,' she said, trying not to pant too loudly. 'I was out of line, too.'

'I don't know what got into me,' he went on. 'I've been acting like an idiot.'

'It's OK,' she puffed. 'I'm not normally so hot-headed either.'

The silence was measured by the sound of his feet running on the treadmill.

'What time are you finishing here?' he asked.

Georgie looked at the digital time readout. *Seven minutes! Was that all she'd done?* 'Um…in about fifty-three minutes,' she answered.

'Do you want to grab a quick bite of dinner somewhere?'

She turned and looked at him, her arms and legs coming to a halt on the machine. 'You mean on a *date*?' she squeaked.

He frowned at her bug-eyed expression. 'Well, sort of, I guess. Is that going to be a problem for you?'

She blew out her pink cheeks and restarted her programme, surreptitiously upping her level. 'I'm supposed to be on a dating fast,' she confessed. 'I made a promise to my flatmate, Rhiannon.'

'You don't have to tell her,' he suggested. 'Anyway, it's just dinner. It's not as if I'm going to go down on bended knee or something. I often have a meal with my registrars.'

Georgie mulled it over in her mind. Dinner with a colleague wasn't really a date, was it? It was more of a professional face to face. 'OK,' she said, sending him a tiny half-smile. 'But I'd appreciate it if you didn't tell anyone at the hospital. I wouldn't want anyone to jump to conclusions.'

'They won't hear about it from me,' Ben said, and upped his level.

Georgie sneaked a look at the level he'd chosen. *Twenty! Surely he wasn't that fit?* She blew out a breath and soldiered on, her legs and arms feeling like lead weights as each minute crawled by.

Ben hardly broke a sweat, she noticed with a twinge of resentment. No doubt all that testosterone gave him an edge. Life certainly wasn't fair when it came to femininity and fitness, she thought with another quick glance at his readout details.

'I'm off for a quick shower,' he said as the last few seconds of her programme were counting down. 'Shall I meet you in Reception or the car park?'

'Reception,' she said, stepping off the machine. 'I jogged down this evening.'

A frown brought his dark brows together. 'Is that safe?' he asked.

'It's only a few blocks from my apartment,' she pointed out.

'Yes, but you can't be too careful,' he said, 'especially at night.'

'You're starting to sound like my father,' she said with a rueful twist to her mouth. 'He thinks I need a bodyguard and has even offered to pay for one.'

A brief flash of annoyance passed over his features at her comment. 'I'll see you in about ten minutes,' he said. 'Or do you need longer?'

Georgie gave him a pert look. 'It takes time to put on lipstick, Mr Blackwood.'

His eyes held hers for a pulsating moment.

'Right, then,' he said, heading towards the male change rooms. 'I'll give you twelve minutes.'

Georgie dived into the shower, quickly shampooing her hair and combing through some conditioner. She dried herself off and dressed in the fresh casual clothes she'd brought in her backpack. She didn't have any make-up with her but she did have a little tub of strawberry flavoured lip-gloss which she dabbed on her lips. She gave her hair a quick blast with the hairdryer on the wall and, finger-combing it into place, walked out to reception.

Ben looked up as she approached, his stomach giving a short, sharp kick of reaction at the sight of her glossy mid-length hair lying loosely about her shoulders. His fingers started to twitch with the impulse to run through the shiny strands and he had to clench his hands to deaden the urge. She was wearing white cotton drawstring trousers and a low-cut T-shirt that hugged her small but firm breasts lovingly. Her waist was tiny and her arms slim and toned, the hint of a golden tan giving her skin a healthy glow. He couldn't remember a time when he'd seen a more naturally beautiful woman.

Desire, hot and urgent, pulsed through him as his gaze

dropped to her mouth. Her lips were plump and glossy, just begging to be kissed.

God, it had been so long since he'd felt a woman's soft touch. He could almost feel the gentle glide of Georgie's smooth hands over his body, touching him, her soft pouting mouth tasting him.

'Everything OK?' she asked, looking up at him.

Ben gave himself a mental shake and smiled. 'Yeah, sorry, I was thinking about something else.'

She fell into step beside him as he led the way outside. 'It's like that, isn't it?' she said. 'Work plays on your mind so much you don't have room for anything else.'

He glanced down at her, breathing in the sweet fresh fragrance of her shampoo, her shoulder brushing against his arm as she moved past him in the doorway. 'Yes, it's amazing how any of us turn out normal when you think about the punishing hours we have to put in,' he said.

He opened the passenger side of his utility for her and wondered if she'd turn up her nose at the faint smell of lucerne hay from his weekend down at the farm.

'Hang on a tick,' he said, reaching past her to shove some feed bills aside. 'There you go.'

'Thank you,' Georgie said as she got in. 'Wow, this is cool. Do you have a farm?'

He got in the driver's side before he answered. 'My mother and stepfather run a property at Mudgee. Cattle mostly, although they've got a few vines in for a wine-maker further up the road. Normally they'd be growing feed crops but the drought has hit them hard.'

She turned to look at him. 'Did you grow up in the bush?'

'Yep.'

'How often do you go out to the property?'

'I try to get out there once a month at least,' he answered.

'Sometimes I manage twice a month but that's not always possible with private practice commitments.'

'Are you going to continue as a staff neurosurgeon or make a total move to the private sector?' she asked.

He changed gear as he headed out into the stream of traffic. 'The financial rewards of private practice are very tempting, but I can't help feeling the public system deserves support. I juggle both with the hours I have available. I enjoy working in a large teaching hospital and, to me, research is a high priority.'

'What's the focus of your research?' Georgie asked, her gaze drifting to his hands, her stomach giving a little kick of reaction as he changed gear again.

'Improving outcomes in cerebral aneurysm,' he answered. 'I'm looking at a couple of different methods of reducing cerebral metabolic requirements in patients with leaking aneurysms, pre-, peri- and post-operatively, to look at outcome improvements. I have some suggestions for a research project for you if you haven't already thought of anything.'

'I have a few ideas,' she said, dragging her eyes away from those long, tanned fingers. 'Ultimately I'm interested in paediatric neurosurgery, but one of my ideas might tie in with your project.'

He flicked a sideways glance her way. 'Is that where you intend to eventually end up—paediatrics?'

'Yes,' she said. 'I love kids, I always have. I guess it's because I'm an only child. I would have loved brothers and sisters.'

'What was your research idea?' he asked.

'Once, when I was an intern, I saw a kid brought in from a yacht. He'd gone overboard, had had a life-jacket on, but had been in the water nearly an hour before he could be retrieved. He'd been bashed in the back of the head, and had been unconscious when he'd gone overboard, and was seriously hypothermic when they had eventually pulled him out.

His CT had shown severe cerebral oedema and his ICPs were through the roof—although he had a pulse, there was no blood pressure and everyone thought he was brain dead, and he actually had a flat EEG. It was forty-eight hours after the accident by the time he was hooked up to a ventilator in ICU. Anyway, he was warmed up, and everyone was expecting a brain-dead organ donor but to everyone's amazement he woke up and eventually was extubated with no subsequent neurologic deficit. It got me to thinking about how the hypothermia may have protected his brain from the neuro insult.'

'That's very interesting,' he said, glancing at her again. 'One of my proposals is to randomly assign leaking aneurysm patients to standard therapy, or induction of hypothermia on admission, prior to, during and for forty-eight hours after aneurysm, clipping, and looking at a range of outcome parameters. Would you be interested in helping to run that project?'

'Yes, I would,' she said, sending him a small smile.

'Great,' he said, and returned to concentrating on finding a parking spot. 'Perhaps we can get together during the next couple of days to fine-tune the details. But for now I'm starving. Is Italian food OK with you?'

'I'm easy,' Georgie said, and then realising what she'd inadvertently inferred, gave a little grimace and added hastily, 'Er...I mean, that's great.'

Ben just smiled as he came around to open her door.

CHAPTER SIX

THE Italian restaurant he had chosen was small but full of the delicious aromas of garlic and basil and home-cooked pasta. It was run by an Italian couple in their late fifties, Gina and Roberto, who greeted Ben warmly as he came in with Georgie a step or two behind.

'*Buona sera*, Dottore Blackwood. Is this your new lady friend? And about time, too. We have been waiting for this for months. Leila Ingham was not pretty enough for you. This one *magnifico!*'

'She's my new registrar, actually,' Ben said, clearly bursting the restaurateur's bubble. 'Georgie, this is Roberto and Gina Di Copella.'

'*Piacare di conoscerla*,' Georgie said with a friendly smile.

'*Parlate Italiano!*'

Georgie rocked her hand back and forth in a gesture of modesty. 'A little.'

Ben waited until they were seated and drinks ordered before he said, 'I didn't realise you were a bit of a linguist. That must come in handy at times.'

'My parents paid for me to go on a six-week holiday to Italy when I finished high school,' she said. 'Then I went to France for a month after I finished medical school. Dad's promised me a month in Switzerland once I finish neurosurgery.'

Ben thought of how he'd had to juggle three part-time jobs just to keep himself enrolled at university. There had been no all-expenses-paid holidays, he hadn't really had a day off the whole time he had been studying. He'd barely had time to sleep. Did she have any idea how the other half lived? he wondered.

'I suppose you went to a private school, huh?' he asked.

Georgie searched his face for a moment. 'Yes, I did,' she answered. 'What about you?'

'No.'

'Why are you looking at me like that?' she asked after a little pause.

'How am I looking at you?'

'Is it my fault I was born into a wealthy background?' she asked with a little frown.

'No, but you need to be aware that others haven't had it as easy as you,' he said. 'In your father's day university was free— anybody could go as long as they had the academic ability, even those from poorer backgrounds. The graduates of today from every faculty are left with massive debts even before they get started in their chosen career. It more or less rules out a tertiary education for people from less affluent backgrounds.'

'I'm quite aware of how hard it is for other people,' she said. 'But my parents have made a lot of sacrifices to give me the things they want to give me, things they didn't have when they were my age.'

He gave a little grunt of cynicism and muttered under his breath, but still loud enough for her to hear it, 'Yeah, like a Porsche and a penthouse.'

Georgie pointedly ignored his comment to ask, 'Who is Leila?'

His blue eyes showed no hint of emotion but Georgie could see how his jaw visibly tightened, a tiny jackhammer of tension tapping beneath the skin near his mouth. 'No one important,' he answered as he turned his attention to the menu in his hands.

'You were in love with her?' The question was out before she could pull it back.

His eyes met hers, a flicker of warning lurking in the dark blue depths. 'I make it a habit to refrain from discussing my love life or lack thereof with my registrars,' he said.

'I didn't mean to pry,' she said with a little pout. 'I just thought you might like to talk about it…you know, to help you get over it.'

He put the menu to one side and, leaning his forearms on the table, pinned her gaze with his. 'I *am* over it, Dr Willoughby. Thank you for your concern but it is not needed or indeed welcome.'

She screwed up her mouth at him. 'I thought we'd progressed past the formality of official titles or are you trying to intimidate me just because I hit on a raw nerve?'

'I don't have any raw nerves, and if I refer to you formally it's only to remind you of our professional relationship in case you get any ideas of stepping over the boundaries.'

Her eyes widened in affront. 'You think that I'm coming on to *you*?'

His brows hooked upwards wryly. 'Aren't you?'

'Of course not!' she said, hot colour staining her cheeks. 'I wouldn't dream of getting involved with someone like you.'

'Too country for your tastes, Geor-gi-a-na?' he asked with a curl of his lip.

She frowned heavily at his mocking pronunciation of her name. 'That's not what I meant at all.'

He picked up the wine list and turned slightly in his chair, which afforded her a view of his broad shoulder instead of his face. 'I expect your father's approval would have to be factored in when choosing a potential partner.' He put the wine list down again and added, 'It wouldn't do to upset him in case he took it on himself to take back his Porsche or penthouse, not to mention the business-class, all-expenses-paid overseas holidays, now, would it?'

Georgie was almost speechless with anger. 'Careful, Mr Blackwood, your country bumpkin complex is showing,' she bit out through tight lips.

His dark eyes flared with anger at her jibe. 'It's true though, isn't it? He would have a coronary if you got involved with someone like me.'

'That's not true,' Georgie said, but without the strength of conviction necessary to convince him. She saw the scepticism in his expression but before she could say anything else Gina came over to take their orders.

'Would you like some wine?' Roberto came over to ask once his wife had left. 'I have a cabernet shiraz that is *eccellente*.'

'Just one glass for me,' Georgie said with a smile.

'And you, Dottore Blackwood?' Roberto addressed Ben.

'The same, thanks, Roberto,' he answered, adding, once Roberto had joined his wife in the kitchen, 'I had better keep a clear head in case I run into trouble on the road tomorrow.'

Georgie sent him a reproachful look. 'Do you have to refer to that incident at every opportunity?'

'I figure that since you're now living in the same vicinity it wouldn't hurt for me to be hyper-vigilant in future,' he said breaking off a piece of garlic bread and popping it into his mouth.

She glared at him heatedly. 'For your information I have a perfect driving record. I haven't even got a parking ticket.'

'None that you would have paid for yourself in any case,' he said as he broke off another piece of bread.

Georgie flashed her eyes at him again. 'What is that supposed to mean?'

He made her wait for his answer by taking his time chewing and swallowing. 'You drive a top-model Porsche and you live in a penthouse. I know registrars earn a heck of a lot in overtime but not enough to fund the sort of lifestyle you're living.'

'You know nothing about my lifestyle,' she shot back.

'Did you pay for your car yourself?'

Georgie set her mouth. 'It was a birthday present but that's none of your—'

'What about the apartment?' he cut her off with a mocking tone. 'Was that a birthday present, too?'

Georgie could feel her fingers on the stem of her glass tightening and lowering her voice so the Italian couple wouldn't hear, ground out through clenched teeth, 'You don't know how close you are to wearing a full glass of red wine.'

His eyes clashed with hers, one edge of his mouth tilting in a you-wouldn't-dare smile. 'That's hardly the sort of behaviour a professor's daughter should display in public, now, is it?'

'Your behaviour is the problem, not mine,' she returned. 'You seem intent on deliberately picking a fight at every opportunity which I can only assume is because of a puerile attempt on your part to vicariously get back at my father for failing you in your fellowship.'

Ben's brows snapped together. 'I suppose you've discussed me at length with him, have you?'

'No,' she said. 'I haven't even told him yet you're my boss.'

'I know exactly what he'll say if and when you do,' he said. 'He'll tell you I'm a country hick with hay stuck between my teeth and a slack attitude to study.'

'If my father failed you, he would have only done so

because he believed you weren't up to the required standard at the time,' Georgie said.

Ben leaned forward with his elbows on the table. 'He failed me because he was a bigoted snob who didn't like the fact that I had the guts to stand up to him, instead of simpering about in his exalted presence like the rest of my peers.'

Georgie had to clamp her mouth over her stinging retort when Gina appeared with their food. She gave the Italian woman a smile that stretched her mouth uncomfortably.

Once Gina had bustled away again Ben broke the brittle silence. 'If your father didn't tell you about my history with him, who did?'

'Richard DeBurgh,' she answered, as she picked up her cutlery. 'And, like me, he thinks you're being petty and childish about harping on about it.'

Ben's lip lifted. 'Oh, does he, now?'

'Yes.'

'So you're pretty chummy with him, are you?'

'I only met him for the first time today so I'd hardly call us best friends but, unlike you, he was nothing but helpful and encouraging towards me.'

'I hate to burst your feminine ego bubble but he's helpful and encouraging to all the female registrars,' he said. 'The only trouble, of course, is he's married, so if you are thinking of upping your chances of a good report from him by sleeping with him, you'd better think again.'

Georgie put down her cutlery with a noisy clatter. 'That's a disgusting assumption to make, not only about him but me as well.'

His held her challenging glare. 'So you're pretty choosy, huh?' he asked.

She picked up her fork and gave her ravioli a little jab. 'I have certain standards, yes,' she answered.

'Lots of money being one of them, I take it.'

Georgie pursed her mouth as she met his taunting look. 'You have a rather poor opinion of women, don't you? Money is not an issue for me, neither is it for a lot of women. What women want in this day and age is a man who is reliable, faithful and not afraid of showing how much he cares for her. If I found a man like that, I wouldn't care if he earned half my wage or even a quarter.'

'You wouldn't have to, given your wealthy background,' he pointed out cynically. 'Your father could top up the bank account for you any time you asked.'

She put down her cutlery again and this time got to her feet as well. 'I can see this is going to be a complete waste of time and food, sitting here with you,' she said. 'I thought the last man I went on a date with was bad but you've taken dates from hell down to a whole new level.'

He leaned back in his chair indolently. 'If you recall, we aren't technically on a date,' he reminded her coolly.

Georgie was momentarily stuck for a retort.

'Are you going to sit down and eat that or not?' he asked, indicating her barely touched food.

She put her hand on her hip and glared at him. 'I suppose this is the part where you give me the boy from the poor background lecture on wasting perfectly good food, is it?'

'No,' Ben said. 'This is the part where I tell you that unless you sit down and finish that meal, Gina and Roberto will feel incredibly insulted. They're nice people and have worked hard to build up this restaurant and will take it personally if you walk out without doing justice to what they prepared for you.'

A battle seemed to be playing out on her face but in the end she blew out a breath and sat down again, her expression stormy as she resumed eating almost mechanically, as if she couldn't wait to get away from his presence.

He watched her as she chomped and chewed, her toffee-brown gaze clashing with his from time to time, twin pools of pink on her cheeks.

He let the silence throb for a few more minutes before he broke it with, 'Tell me more about this dating embargo you're on. How did that come about?'

She gave a little grimace as she dabbed at the corners of her mouth with her napkin. 'My flatmate and I have had the most appallingly bad luck with men,' she said. 'We decided to make a pact to see if we could stay the distance. Three months with no official dates. If one of us breaks the deal we have to pay one thousand dollars.'

'Have you found it hard so far?'

She gave him an ironic look. 'It's only the second week of January so, no, not at all.'

'Will that be the longest you've been without male company?' he asked.

Georgie tried to read his expression but could make little of it. 'I'm not a serial dater if that's what you're implying,' she said. 'For one thing I've been studying for the last nine years so that has been my main focus. What about you? How long has it been since you broke up with Leila?'

'I can't really remember,' he said, shifting his gaze from hers. 'Nine months or so, I guess.'

'Have you dated anyone since?'

His eyes moved back to meet hers. 'You're the first,' he said with a rueful look, 'although technically this isn't a date.'

'No…of course it isn't,' Georgie said, trying not to stare at his well-shaped mouth for too long.

'So, Dr Willoughby,' he said with a hint of a smile, 'your thousand dollars is still safe.'

Not as safe as I'd like it to be, Georgie thought. God, he was so gorgeous when he smiled like that. His midnight-blue eyes crinkled up at the corners and his features relaxed, giving him a laid-back, devil-may-care demeanour that was totally irresistible.

Her stomach did a rapid tumble turn when she thought of how it would feel to have those firm lips pressed to hers, the stroke and glide of his tongue parting the shield of her lips to hunt down and mate with hers. Desire began to crawl over her skin, making it lift and tighten all over. The tender spot between her thighs began to pulse with longing to feel the thick invasion of his male presence, his rock-hard abdomen slick with sweat as it pinned hers beneath him in the most intimate way possible…

'Have I got spinach in my teeth or something?' he asked, jerking her away from her traitorous thoughts.

'Er…no…' she said, desperately trying to control the steady creep of colour in her cheeks.

'You were staring at my mouth.'

She feigned a guileless look. 'Was I?'

'Yes.'

Georgie forced her gaze to hold his teasing one. 'I guess you're pretty used to having women stare at you all the time but, let me assure you, in this case it had nothing whatsoever to do with your physical attributes. I was thinking about something else entirely.'

'What were you thinking about?'

She looked at him for a moment while her brain hunted for a lie. 'Um…dessert,' she said, mentally congratulating herself for finding something that was at least partially true. 'I was thinking of what I could have for dessert.'

His eyes dipped to her mouth before returning to hers, a cryptic little smile turning up the edges of his mouth. 'So was I,' he said, and handed her the menu, his fingers brushing against hers.

CHAPTER SEVEN

GEORGIE buried her head in the menu, her fingers still tingling where Ben's had touched hers. She was ashamed at her weakness. She had been so confident she would win the bet with Rhiannon but she could see that things were going to get tricky if she didn't put a stop to this right now. She couldn't remember a time when she had been so instantly attracted to a man. Sure, she'd had a few boyfriends, and Andrew McNally, the last one, had been relatively serious. She had even considered herself in love enough to contemplate marriage until she had found out his previous girlfriend hadn't quite moved out of his life.

Georgie realised that it had been her pride that had taken the beating, not her heart. But falling in love with Ben Blackwood was not just going to lose her a thousand dollars. He had a chip on his shoulder that was going to take quite some shifting and she wasn't sure she was up to the task of doing it.

Besides, she was supposed to be focusing on her career, not marriage and babies, although the thought of a baby with dark blue eyes was certainly very tempting. So, too, was the method of conceiving one…

'What have you decided?'

Georgie looked at him blankly. 'What?'

He indicated the menu in her hands. 'Dessert,' he said. 'Are you a gelato girl or a cheesecake chick?'

She looked back at the menu, this time actually reading what was printed there. 'It's a toss-up between the cheesecake and the chocolate mousse,' she said, suddenly feeling self-conscious under his steady gaze.

'We could get both and share,' he suggested.

She closed the menu and met his eyes across the table. Sharing a dessert seemed a little bit intimate but, then, so too did the fact that they were now the only people in the restaurant. The lights were low, the background music soft and romantic—even the single red rose on the table added to the atmosphere of courtship.

'Maybe I'll just have coffee,' she said. 'I'm on call again tomorrow from eight in the morning so I might have to cut my gym class short.'

'I hardly think you'd need to bother about excess calories,' he said as he closed the menu. 'You've got a BMI of about nineteen.'

'I hope you're not implying I'm too thin,' she said with a quelling glance. 'I'm in the normal weight range for my height.'

His eyes went to the slight swell of her breasts before coming back to mesh with hers. 'It's an addiction, you know.'

'What?' she asked with a pert tilt of her head. 'Looking at women leeringly?'

His dark blue eyes glinted. 'Exercise,' he said. 'People get high on the endorphins. They can't go a day without working out or they get agitated and edgy.'

'I can assure you I have no such addiction,' she said with a little toss of her head. 'I just enjoy the thinking time it gives me, as well as the cardiovascular fitness. Anyway, what about you?' Her eyes ran over his toned upper body. 'Your body

mass index is probably just as low and your percentage body
fat percentage is certainly below mine.'

'That's true, but I try and keep a healthy balance between
work commitments and exercise,' he said. 'Pushing your body
to the limits all the time is damaging in the long term. Besides,
the hours we work are punishing enough, without overload-
ing the body with even more stress.'

'Thank you for the advice but I am not a gym junkie with
no respect for my own well-being,' she said. 'I do actually
know how to look after myself. I am a doctor, remember.'

'Was it your choice to do neurosurgery or something your
father expected you to do?' he asked a few moments later
when Roberto had brought them their coffees.

'It was my choice,' she said. 'From when I was young I
loved hearing about my father's work. I was fascinated with
neurosurgery, the delicacy of it, the skill and dedication it
takes to become highly competent. I never considered
anything other than following in his footsteps, although, as I
said earlier, I see myself in paediatrics eventually.'

'So what about marriage and babies?' he asked as he stirred
his coffee. 'Is that part of your overall plan?'

She toyed with the handle of her cup with her fingers, her
eyes shifting away from his. 'Like every other career-woman,
I'm a little worried I might end up childless because of circumstances beyond my control.'

'Circumstances such as what?'

Her eyes met his briefly. 'Well, I've got another four years
of study, meaning I'll be thirty-one when I finish. So if I haven't
found a partner by my mid-thirties who is also keen to have
children straight away, fertility issues might be a problem.'

'It's certainly a problem most professional women have to
face,' he agreed. 'But you could always suspend your training
if you wanted to. That's at least one option female trainees in

years past didn't have the opportunity to do. The Australasian College of Surgeons has become one of the most progressive in the world for facilitating surgical training for women.'

'I know,' she said. 'And I would do it if the right man came along but I don't see that happening any time soon.'

'Ah such cynicism in one so young,' he drawled. 'Maybe your standards are a little too high. Have you considered that possibility?'

She gave him an arctic look. 'No, and I have no intention of lowering them. I don't think it's unreasonable to expect a man to treat me with respect and deep and abiding love for the term of our natural lives.'

'So you're a romantic, are you?' he asked.

'No more than the average woman.'

'Are your parents happily married?'

Georgie hesitated for a fraction of a second before she answered him. Her mother gave the appearance of being perfectly content with the luxurious life her position as the non-working wife of a very successful man afforded her, but Georgie often wondered if she filled her days with bridge games and book club meetings in an effort to make up for the loneliness of enduring a marriage that had not been an overtly affectionate one. She couldn't remember a single time when her parents had kissed in front of her, apart from a rather formal peck on the cheek whenever her father had left on one of his overseas conferences. She hadn't even seen them hold hands in public. They shared a bedroom but that, of course, didn't necessarily mean their relationship was still a physical one.

'They're still together after thirty years,' she finally said.

'You didn't really answer my question.'

'That's because it's none of your business.'

He smiled at her pert expression. 'You don't need to get all prickly, Georgie,' he said. 'To tell you the truth, I'm a bit of a romantic myself. I'm a great believer in the institution of marriage. My mother has been married twice, and very happily, too.'

'You mentioned you have a stepfather,' Georgie said. 'Does that mean your own father died?'

A shadow flitted over his face but disappeared just as quickly. 'Yeah,' he said, shifting his gaze a fraction. 'I was six years old.'

'What happened?' she asked softly.

His eyes came back to hers, the flicker of pain in their bluer than blue depths striking at the tender core of Georgie's heart. 'Tractor accident,' he said in an emotionless tone that she instinctively knew was a facade. 'It rolled when a part of the bank he was driving on collapsed.'

'That must have been truly devastating for you and your mother and your sister,' she said.

He looked at her, his eyes narrowing slightly. 'I don't recall telling you I had a sister,' he said. 'Have you been discussing me with the staff?'

Georgie felt her face start to heat. 'Jennifer Patterson in A and E mentioned you had a sister who'd been injured in an accident,' she explained. 'I wasn't searching for information, if that's what you're thinking.'

'She's my half-sister,' he said after a small but taut silence.

'How old is she?'

'She turned sixteen a few weeks ago.'

Georgie ran her tongue over the dryness of her lips. 'Is she OK now?'

His eyes met hers again. 'Yes. She made a complete recovery. She's a good kid, works hard at school and loves horses and the usual girl stuff. She's coming to stay with me this weekend. It's my mother and stepfather's anniversary so I thought I'd offer to take Hannah to the beach and do some shopping.'

Georgie felt her antagonism towards him melt like ice cream under the force of a blowtorch. He sounded like the perfect big brother, adoring, supportive and affectionate. She could hear it in his voice, the love he had for his sister, and it made her wonder if she had been a little too hasty in her judgement of him.

She fidgeted with her coffee-cup again, her eyes not quite managing to meet his. 'I...I feel very bad about what happened yesterday,' she began awkwardly, 'you know, me knocking you off your bike like that. I didn't really apologise properly and when I heard what had happened to your sister and the patient you had three weeks ago I started to understand why you had been so...so...'

'Forget it,' he said. 'No lasting damage was done.'

She bit her lip as she lifted his gaze back to his. 'You're being very gracious about it. You have a perfect right to be annoyed. I should have looked before I opened the door but I was in a hurry to get to the hospital and...well, you know the rest.'

'It's fine, Georgie,' he said. 'I shouldn't have treated you the way I did. I can assure you it's not my usual style at all.'

She smiled at him tentatively. 'So you really are the laid back nice guy everyone told me you were?'

He smiled back at her, the whiteness of his teeth against the tan of his face making her realise all over again how very attractive he was. 'I'm not an overbearing ogre,' he said. 'But I do have high standards when it comes to the care of patients. I have a responsibility to train you and as long as you are prepared to work hard, I'm sure we'll get along just fine.'

'In spite of who my father is?' she asked with a little arch of one brow.

He held her look for a lengthy moment, his smile slowly fading. 'I realise that it's often hard for a family member to understand or even recognise the issues other people have with the ones they love. Your father is what I would consider a difficult personality, but that's not to say he isn't a good father. After all, even the world's most murderous dictators still went home and hugged their own children.'

Georgie felt her hackles begin to rise all over again. 'I'm not sure I like the idea of my father being compared to a murderous dictator.'

'Would you agree he is at times a difficult person to deal with?'

'No, of course not,' she said. 'My father has always been wonderfully supportive and easy to get along with.'

'That's probably because you've got him wrapped around your little finger,' he said. 'You only have to speak to a few of the theatre staff who've worked with him in the past to find out he was an arrogant, bombastic, instrument-throwing tyrant when things didn't go his way. I certainly hope you're not going to follow suit for I will not tolerate it.'

She gritted her teeth, fighting the urge to toss the contents of her coffee-cup in his face. 'You really can't help yourself, can you?' she asked.

His eyes went to the white-knuckled grip she had on her cup before returning to her flashing brown eyes. 'Rule number one, Dr Willoughby,' he said. 'If you throw that coffee in my face, you will be off the training scheme so fast you won't know what hit you.'

Georgie got to her feet so abruptly her thighs bumped the edge of the table, sending the contents of her cup straight into his lap. She swallowed in horror as the dark stain spread, her heart thumping irregularly as the silence began to thicken the air until breathing became difficult.

He slowly got to his feet, his expression rigid with anger as he mopped up the spillage with his napkin.

'I—I'm sorry,' she said. 'I didn't mean to do that.'

His eyes cut to hers. 'Didn't you?'

'Of course not. It was an accident.'

He tossed the soiled napkin on the table. 'You seem very good at attracting accidents, don't you, Dr Willoughby?'

'Is everything all right?' Gina asked as she came back in.

Ben turned to face the Italian woman with a reassuring smile. 'It's OK, Gina,' he said, 'just a little accident. I'll settle the bill and take Dr Willoughby home before we do any more damage.'

'You are both tired from working all day,' Gina said as she cleared the table. 'You doctors are all the same. Working, working, working.'

Georgie waited until Gina had gone to fetch the bill before saying, 'I'd like to pay my share.'

'No.'

She frowned at him. 'What do you mean, no?'

'I asked you out for a meal so I pay. That's rule number two.'

She folded her arms and waited while he paid the bill. After saying their goodbyes to Gina and Roberto, he escorted her out to his car, his hand at her elbow a little too forceful for her liking. She tried to edge away but he was having none of it. His fingers tightened as he swung her round to face him.

'What are you doing?' she asked as his pelvis brushed against hers.

His dark brooding gaze locked down on hers. 'You're rather attached to the stuck-up-little-princess role, aren't you?' he asked.

She tossed her hair back with a flicking movement of her head. 'I am nothing of the sort. *You*, on the other hand, are performing rather brilliantly the role of the overbearing boss.'

His mouth lifted in a smirk. 'I bet you're expecting me to kiss you right now. I can see it in your eyes. That's how it goes, isn't it, Georgie? Seduce the difficult boss so he gives you a glowing report at the end of your term.'

She looked at him in outrage, her face flaming with colour. 'I'd rather kiss a cane toad,' she bit out.

He laughed and pulled her even closer, the dampness of his coffee-soaked groin seeping through the thin cotton of her drawstring trousers. 'Have you ever kissed a cane toad?' he asked.

Georgie felt her heart begin to leap about in her chest. She had to get out of his arms before she was tempted to press even closer to his hard warmth. 'Let me go.'

Ben's eyes went to her mouth, the temptation to lower his to cover its soft pouting contours almost overwhelming. He could feel his body stirring, the hot surge of pulsing blood making him feel like throwing caution to the winds and offering her a brief fling just for the heck of it. He didn't think it would take too much to convince her to sleep with him. She was clearly fighting her attraction to him, as he was to her. He could feel it every time they touched, the current of sexual energy like the zap of a laser gun. Her body was so close to his he could feel the outline of her feminine mound, the thought of cupping it in his hand and exploring her with his fingers almost tipping him out of the bounds of self-control.

'If you do not let me go this instant, I will open my mouth and scream so loudly the police will hear it out at Parramatta,' she threatened, with flashing eyes.

Ben had no reason to believe she wouldn't do it. She was a feisty little thing and the last thing he needed was a trumped-up assault charge thrown at him to ruin his reputation. He dropped his hands from her arms and stepped back from her.

'I'll make my own way home,' she said with an imperious hitch of her chin.

'Rule number three is I make sure you return home safely.' He opened the car door and nodded his head towards the passenger seat. 'Get in.'

Georgie stood her ground. 'Get lost,' she shot back, and then added insultingly, 'Anyway, I don't want to get dirty in that stupid farm car of yours with its bits of hay and smell of cows. I'm going to get a cab.'

His jaw locked with anger as he watched her stalk to a cab parked a short distance away. *Stuck-up, little city-girl snob*, he thought. Slamming the passenger door of his utility, he strode around to the driver's side, still muttering under his breath as he arrived at his apartment block ten minutes later.

CHAPTER EIGHT

'Gosh, whatever happened to your brand new trousers?' Rhiannon asked as soon as Georgie came in later that night.

Georgie looked down at the brown stain on the front of her white cotton drawstring trousers, a funny sensation passing deep and low through her belly at the thought of how it had got there. 'Um…I spilt my coffee.'

Rhiannon's eyes narrowed suspiciously. 'Who'd you have coffee with?'

Georgie avoided her friend's piercing gaze by making a show of emptying her gym bag. 'It wasn't a date so stop looking at me like that,' she said.

'So who was it? Someone from the gym?'

'It was my boss.'

'That's all right, then,' Rhiannon said, folding her arms. 'He doesn't count.'

Georgie turned to look at her. 'What do you mean, he doesn't count?'

'He's not your soul mate.'

This time is was Georgie who narrowed her eyes. 'Have you been talking to Madame Celestia about me again?'

Rhiannon gave her a sheepish look. 'I happened to run into her buying a book on anger management at Bondi Junction Plaza.'

'So she's not a happy medium, then?' Georgie quipped.

Rhiannon pursed her mouth. 'Joke all you like, Georgie. Anyway, I mentioned how you'd had an accident yesterday and she warned me that with the current alignment of the planets in your star sign you could very well have another one, and soon.'

Georgie would have rolled her eyes but she suddenly remembered what had happened that morning on the way to work. 'I was at the scene of an accident this morning but it was nothing but a coincidence,' she said. 'That strip of road is notorious for minor prangs, especially during peak hour.'

Rhiannon's eyes went wide. 'You see? I told you it's not a joking matter. Madame Celestia *does* have special powers.'

Georgie flopped down on the sofa, laid her head back on the cushioned softness and closed her eyes wearily. 'I wish she did, then I could ask her to make my life a little easier by making Ben Blackwood less prejudiced against me.'

Rhiannon sat next to her on the sofa, her legs tucked beneath her. 'Is he still giving you a hard time?'

'I can't quite make him out,' Georgie said as she sat back upright and opened her eyes to look at her friend. 'He turned up at the gym this evening and apologised for a misunderstanding we'd had earlier, but then all the way through dinner he kept chipping away at me about my background. He thinks I'm a rich snob, I know he does.'

'Yeah, well, you do drive a Porsche and live in a beachside penthouse paid for by your father,' Rhiannon pointed out.

'I know, but what's the point of having a child if you don't share your wealth with them?' Georgie argued. 'Besides, I wanted to move out to give Mum a chance to rebalance her relationship with Dad.'

'So, this dinner you had with your boss,' Rhiannon said with a probing look. 'Are you sure that wasn't a date by any chance?'

'Very definitely not,' Georgie insisted.

Her flatmate leaned a little closer. 'Did he kiss you?' she asked.

Georgie felt her cheeks storming with colour. 'For God's sake, Rhiannon, surely you don't think I would consider having a fling with my boss.' *Oh, yes, you would!* a little voice piped up in her head, but she quickly shut it out.

'Is he nice-looking?'

'Yes, but—'

'And he's not gay?'

Georgie recalled the hardened probe of Ben's body as he'd held her close. 'Er…no, very definitely not gay.'

Rhiannon inspected her crimson-painted fingernails for a moment. 'You know, Georgie, we could always call off the anti-dating deal, if that's what you want.'

Georgie stared at her. 'Have *you* found someone?' she asked.

'Of course not!' Rhiannon said, flushing slightly. 'I just thought we should have thought about the possibility that someone truly decent might come along and if we didn't respond to their interest we might miss out on our only chance at happiness.'

'I guess you're right,' Georgie said, releasing another little sigh. 'But so far I haven't met anyone I want to spend the rest of the year with, let alone the rest of my life.'

'You have to spend a year with this Ben Blackwood guy though, don't you?'

Georgie gave a groan. 'Don't remind me.'

Rhiannon just smiled.

Georgie was just coming out of the gym at seven-fifty-nine the next morning when her mobile phoned beeped, indicating an incoming message. She checked the screen and saw

that she had a missed call from A and E. She quickly
called the number and the registrar on duty answered. 'Dr
Willoughby, we've got an MVA down here. Two victims,
husband and wife, both middle-aged. The husband's got some
bumps and bruises, but I think the wife's got an extradural.
She had a GCS of 12 on arrival, with equal pupils, but she's
gone off to GCS 9 over a matter of minutes and her left
pupil's blown up. Can you get down here now and look at
her?'

'I'm on my way, Drew,' she said. 'Can you get Anaesthetics
down now? I'll phone Theatre on my mobile while I'm coming
down.'

'Right.'

Georgie raced to her car and, pushing aside all thoughts
of Madame Celestia's predictions, drove with care but haste
to the hospital.

When she arrived in A and E, Drew Yaxley, the registrar,
quickly filled her in on the patients' conditions.

'The wife's pulse and BP have just hit the floor, Dr
Willoughby. The anaesthetics registrar has intubated her. The
general surgical registrar is just about through the secondary
survey now but it looks like it's pretty much an isolated head
injury. Husband's got minor general surgical trauma—no
neuro injury.'

Georgie came over to where a middle-aged blonde woman
was lying on the emergency trolley, intubated, with Kevin Chase,
the general surgical registrar, completing his examination.

'Georgie, this looks like a neuro emergency,' Kevin
informed her. 'She's got a clinical left skull fracture, and very
little else. ABCs were pretty good when she got here, but her
GCS went off in front of my eyes when I was doing the
primary survey, and she's blown up her left pupil. They were
equal when she first got here. Jane has intubated her, but

she's become bradycardic and hypotensive. I'm pretty sure she's got an extradural.'

'Dr Willoughby, if this is an extradural, you're going to have to do something now,' Jane said, looking stressed as the beeps on the ECG showed a slowing pulse, now down to 40. 'She'll arrest before we get her anywhere near Theatre, let alone CT.'

Georgie examined the patient, noting the boggy haematoma over the left scalp, the dilated left pupil, the hypotension and bradycardia. 'Are you sure she's not hypovolaemic, Kevin? Are there other injuries?' she asked.

'A bit of bruising, but nothing serious, Dr Willoughby. Like I said, she seems to have an isolated left head injury. The ambos said the car ran into a tree on her side.'

'Georgie, if you can do anything here, you'd better do it now. Her pulse is 25 and no BP,' Jane said.

'Kevin, get Ben Blackwood on the phone, tell him what's happening and ask him to come in straight away. Tell him I'm doing an emergency burr-hole in A and E. Drew, get your staff to bring the emergency neuro tray, gown and gloves.' She turned to the hovering nurse and instructed, 'Get me some gloves, goggles and a couple of razors to shave the scalp.'

Quickly Georgie turned the woman's head to the right a little and shaved the left scalp. While nursing staff opened up the emergency neuro tray, she quickly gowned and gloved and injected 1 percent xylocaine with adrenaline into the scalp over the left parietal region. She then prepped the scalp with Betadine and used a section drape to isolate the area. She made a 5 cm incision over the scalp down to the periosteum and inserted a self-retaining retractor. She then took the handbrace with attached skull bit and started drilling into bone at the site of the now visible skull fracture.

Georgie could feel her skin breaking out in fine beads of perspiration, her tension levels rocketing second by second as she concentrated on the boring. After two or three minutes the centre of the bit breached the inner layer of the skull. She continued to drill for a few more turns to enlarge the hole and then removed the brace. From the hole in the centre of the conical skull defect she had created, fresh arterial blood rapidly flowed out under pressure. She took bone nibblers and enlarged the burr-hole, from which at least 100 ml fresh blood emerged under pressure, slowing to a continuous ooze and revealing the depressed dura underneath.

'You've certainly done something, Dr Willoughby,' Jane said. 'Her pulse has come up to 100 and her BP's now recordable at least.'

Just then the emergency room doors burst open as Ben came in.

'Dr Willoughby, what the hell's going on in here? What the hell are you doing, drilling burr-holes in A and E?' he asked.

Georgie refused to be put off by his overbearing manner. She had done what she had done in the best interests of keeping the patient alive, and so far her actions had worked. 'She was about to arrest, Mr Blackwood,' she said a little coolly. 'She would never have survived a CAT scan or the transfer to Theatre.'

'She's right, Ben,' Jane said. 'Dr Willoughby had to do something there and then or we would have lost the patient. As it is, there's been an instant rebound in her parameters. At least now you've got a live patient to take to Theatre, thanks to your registrar.'

Ben inspected the patient over Georgie's shoulder, his body touching hers from behind. 'It's very uncommon to have to do burr-holes this urgently. But it looks like a good call in this case, Georgie,' he said after a momentary pause. 'That's a decent-looking emergency burr-hole, too. Have you ever done one before?'

'The first burr-hole I've done was in my first theatre list with you two days ago,' Georgie replied, stepping away from the heat of his body.

'Well done, then. That was not only a good call but a brave piece of rare emergency neurosurgery,' he said. Turning to Jane, he asked, 'How are her obs now, Jane?'

'Pulse 100 and BP now 120 over 90. A vast improvement. Her left pupil has come down a bit, but it's still dilated,' Jane answered.

'Georgie, you need to put a suction drain over the burr-hole and staple the scalp closed, get the wound dressed, and get a CT stat so we know what else we're dealing with, then straight up to Theatre,' Ben instructed.

'Theatre's ready—I called them half an hour ago—and CT has been cleared and is waiting for us,' Georgie informed him, still glowing inside from his unexpected praise.

'Well, then, there's nothing left for me to do here. Seems you pretty well have things under control. I'll go and get changed and come down to CT in fifteen minutes. When we take her to Theatre, I want you to do the decompressing flap and I'll assist.'

Georgie opened her mouth to say she wasn't ready to be the primary surgeon but he'd already pushed through the swing doors.

'You'll be fine,' Jane said as she cleared away the used instruments. 'You have to start somewhere, and you've done a good job so far.'

'Thanks,' Georgie said with a weak smile.

She accompanied the patient a short time later to CT Scanning and once the scans were done Ben came in to look at them. He stood at Georgie's shoulder as he inspected each one, now and again brushing against her with his arm as he lifted it to place another scan on the X-ray board. She could smell his lemony aftershave and her gaze drifted to his tanned forearm, the sleeves of his shirt rolled back casually, the dusting of black hair making her skin lift in a tiny shiver as she thought about those arms touching her flesh.

'What do you think the scans show?' he asked as the last one was illuminated.

Georgie moistened her lips and began, 'Um…she's got a depressed left skull fracture and still some extradural clot despite the burr-hole… And there's underlying cerebral contusion.'

'Yeah, I agree. So where do we go from here?'

She stared at the scan until it blurred in front of her eyes. 'She needs the rest of that clot evacuated,' she said.

She waited for him to respond but when she sent her gaze towards him he was looking at the first scan again, a frown drawing his dark brows together.

'Was this the driver?' he asked.

'No, the husband was.'

He looked down at her, still frowning. 'Are you sure?'

'Positive,' she answered. 'It's in the notes.'

He looked back at the scan and rubbed at his chin for a moment. 'What sort of car was it?' he asked. 'Modern? Fitted with airbags, do you know?'

'I'm not sure about that,' she said. 'Why? Do you think there's something fishy about this?'

He turned to look at her again, the frown now smoothed out. 'If there is, no doubt the police will sort it out. But I would prefer it if you didn't mention this to anyone until we have the accident investigation angle on things. Let's get her down to Theatre and clean out that clot.'

After they had scrubbed Ben assisted Georgie through the procedure, raising a temporo-parietal flap, sucking out the residual haematoma and inserting an intracranial pressure monitor.

Even though she was incredibly nervous, Georgie could see why Ben had a reputation for being calm and in control during surgery. He stood by her side, speaking only when necessary and in an encouraging tone in spite of how they had left each other's company the previous evening.

Whenever she met his gaze she felt again the incredible intimacy of working with him in Theatre. The only part of his face she could see was his dark blue eyes, their silent message of reassurance one that made her anger towards him soften around the edges.

He was clearly far too professional to bring petty personal issues into Theatre where patients relied on his skill and dedication. The patient came first and always would, which was something she wouldn't dream of arguing with.

Finally the last staple was in and the patient was transferred to neurosurgical ICU for post-operative monitoring.

'Good job, Georgie,' Ben said as he stripped off his gloves and tossed them in the bin. 'Do you fancy a quick coffee before you hit the ward?'

Georgie searched his face to see if he was mocking her but as far as she could tell his offer seemed genuine. She couldn't, however, help the slip of her gaze to his pelvis, for the first time wondering if the hot liquid had burned him. She decided against asking him in front of the theatre staff, who were cleaning up behind them, and instead moved through to the female change rooms after telling him she would meet him in his office in five minutes.

She pushed open the doors of the change room and came face to face with a woman in her early forties who was dressed in theatre gear.

'Hello, Georgiana,' the woman said. 'I'm Madeleine Brothers, Associate Professor of Neurosurgery. I've been waiting for you to come to my office and introduce yourself to me.'

Georgie did her best to ignore the hint of censure in the woman's tone and offered her hand. 'Hello, Professor Brothers. I'm sorry but I've had a bit of a hectic start to my term. You were next on my list.'

Madeleine briefly shook her hand and gave her a smile that Georgie couldn't help feeling was a little forced. 'How are you getting along with Ben Blackwood?' she asked.

Georgie's tiny hesitation in replying was obviously noted by the older woman, who arched one thin brow speculatively.

'Fine. He's seems…er…very competent.'

'He is,' Madeleine said. 'But, then, he was trained by one of the best—your father.'

'You worked with my father?' Georgie asked.

Madeleine nodded. 'Before I came here I worked at one of the private hospitals your father operated at twice weekly. How is he enjoying being a man of leisure?'

'Like most doctors, he's finding it hard to fill in all the spare time he now has,' Georgie said.

'He could always do a locum in the country or overseas,' Madeleine said. 'It seems a shame to deprive the community of all that talent when he's still perfectly capable of working, even if for fewer hours.'

Georgie decided to see if what Ben had said about her father the night before had any substance to it. 'Did you enjoy working with my father?' she asked.

'Yes, I did,' Madeleine answered without hesitation. 'He was a hard taskmaster certainly, and he didn't suffer fools gladly. But he was a damned good neurosurgeon. I learned a lot from him. I'll always be immensely grateful. He was the one who encouraged me to pursue an academic career. I would never have published as many research papers as I have without his support and direction.'

'I've heard it said he was difficult to work with.'

'Who isn't on a bad day?' Madeleine said. 'Even the notoriously easygoing Ben Blackwood can be like a bear with a sore head if someone rubs him up the wrong way.'

Georgie's mouth formed a little moue. 'Yes, I have sort of noticed that.'

Madeleine moved closer, her voice lowering slightly. 'Look, Georgiana, I know you'll probably think I'm speaking out of turn but I wouldn't want to see you jeopardise your first neurosurgical term here by having an improper relationship with a senior colleague.'

Georgie looked at the older woman in surprise. 'Surely a relationship between two unattached adults is not considered improper?'

'No, you're right. Perhaps I could have rephrased that a little better. But I think I should warn you Ben is still getting over a rather nasty break-up,' Madeleine said. Stretching her lips into another tight little smile, she added, 'I wouldn't like to see the daughter of a man I admire very much get hurt.'

Georgie wondered if Madeleine Brothers's concern had an entirely different motive. She was after all only five or six years older than Ben and as far as she'd heard not married. 'Thank you for your warning me,' she said. 'But I can assure you I have no intention of getting involved with Mr Blackwood.'

'Good,' Madeleine said, as she moved past her to push open the door. 'That would indeed be very wise. He's a bit of a heartbreaker is our Ben. Enjoy your stay with us, Georgiana. No doubt I'll see you in my theatre soon.'

Georgie didn't get the chance to answer as the door swung

shut in her face. She turned and looked at her reflection in the mirror. 'Heartbreaker, is he?' she said out loud. 'Well, not with me, Mr Break-your-heart Blackwood.'

CHAPTER NINE

EN was on the phone when Georgie knocked on his office oor and he called out for her to come in before continuing is conversation with the person on the line. 'I told you it's ne, Mum,' he said. 'I haven't got any commitments this eekend. I'm not on call and the weather's going to be good o just relax and enjoy yourselves.'

Georgie felt a little uncomfortable listening in on what was early a private family conversation. She stood shifting from ne foot to the other, pretending an interest in the books on ne shelves running alongside his desk.

'If it will make you feel a little better, I'll rustle up some emale company for Hannah in case she gets sick of her oring older brother,' he said. 'Shopping is not exactly my rong point but I'm sure I can find someone who will show er where all the best shops are.'

Georgie felt the point between her shoulder blades begin o prickle as if his dark blue gaze had centred there. She eached for a heavy textbook on emergency neurosurgery nd flicked through the step-by-step diagrams.

'Right, then,' he said. 'That's settled. I'll be at the station o meet her at seven on Friday evening. And for pity's sake op worrying. It's about time you and Jack got some time to

yourselves.' There was a little pause and he added affectio
ately, 'Love you, too.'

'Sorry about that,' he said to Georgie as he flipped h
mobile shut. 'My mother is having cold feet about leaving n
in charge of my little sister in the big bad city of Sydney.'

'I'm sure you'll do a wonderful job of chaperoning he
Georgie offered. 'Is she…er, a bit of a rebel or something'

'No, she's not a rebel. She's more of an extrovert. A
mouth, if you know what I mean.'

'If you want some help over the weekend I'd be happy
help,' she said on an impulse she could neither explain n
retract in time. 'I mean…with shopping and stuff…that's
you haven't got anyone else to call on…'

He sat back in his chair, his expression thoughtful as h
eyes caught and held hers. 'That's rather generous of yo
considering how we spoke to each other last night,' he con
mented wryly.

Georgie gave him a shamefaced look. 'I'm really sor
about the coffee incident,' she said. 'I could have scalde
your…er…you.' She moistened her dry lips and added te
tatively, 'Are you…um…all right?'

His eyes began to twinkle. 'My abdomen was pretty r
last night, not blistered, though, probably just first degre
Why don't you give me the once-over and see for yourself'

Her face erupted with heat and so too did her lower body
the thought of examining him intimately. She had seen plen
of male bodies in the nine years of her training but somehow sl
suspected his would be something else entirely. She wouldn
have a hope of maintaining clinical distance—she was havin
a hard enough time reminding herself he was her superior.

'I thought women of your generation didn't know how
blush,' he said, smiling at her. 'You have examined men
groins before, I take it?'

Georgie felt her colour go to an all-time high. 'I thought I was here for a cup of coffee, not a discussion about my history of men's nether regions,' she said in a clipped tone.

He shifted his mouth from side to side in a contemplative manner. 'Leaving my burnt groin aside for the moment, is your offer to help my sister shop a genuine one?'

She was momentarily nudged off course by his rapid change of subject. 'Yes, of course it was,' she answered. 'I love shopping and would be glad to help.'

'Good,' he said. 'What about we meet Saturday morning in the city at the Market Street entrance to the Queen Victoria Building, say, at ten?'

'That would be fine,' she said. 'I'm not on call and I was going shopping anyway.'

'Right, then,' he said as he got to his feet. 'Let's go and chase down a cup of coffee. There's a café just outside the hospital grounds. I don't know about you, but I hate the cafeteria stuff.'

'So only the designer blend will do, huh?' Georgie said with a pert look. 'Don't tell me you're a bit of coffee snob?'

He held her gaze for a couple of beats. 'A cup of decent coffee now and again isn't going to break my budget,' he returned as he held the door open.

Georgie brushed past him in the door, her nostrils widening to take in the clean male scent of him, her stomach clenching and unclenching at the thought of him holding her close as he had last night. Her body could still feel the hard imprint of his. She had lain awake for hours thinking about him, wondering how she was going to cope with working alongside him for a whole year without falling in love with him. She even wondered if she was starting to do so now. Overhearing his conversation with his mother and witnessing the tender concern he had for his sister was enough to melt any hardened female heart.

The café he took her to was a popular coffee chain, one that had opened up recently. It was buzzing with the second-wave morning crowd but they still managed to find a small table at the back once their coffees were ready.

Georgie kept the lid on her latte and the risk of another spill. No doubt second degree burns would be next and an examination mandatory, so she sipped her coffee through the tiny spout instead.

'About last night…' they said in unison.

'You go first,' they said, again in unison.

Georgie looked at him and smiled at exactly the same time as he did. 'I really didn't mean to toss my coffee in your lap like that,' she said. 'I admit I was tempted to throw it in your face but I wouldn't have done it no matter how provocative you were being.'

'Was I being provocative?' he asked with an all-too-innocent look.

She gave him a mock frown. 'You know you were.'

His mouth stretched into a guilty-as-charged grin. 'All right, I admit it. Sorry, but I can't seem to help it. You press all my buttons for some reason.'

Georgie examined the plastic lid of her coffee cup. 'I guess we didn't exactly meet under the best of circumstances,' she said, running the tip of her index finger over the brand name embellished there.

'No, but that doesn't mean we can't have a good working relationship,' he said. 'You did a good job this morning, especially considering your lack of experience.'

Georgie could feel herself glowing again under the warmth of his praise. 'Thank you,' she said. 'I was really nervous.'

'You didn't show it.'

'I was shaking in my shoes.'

'As long as your hands are steady I don't care what your

egs are doing,' he said, and then after a tiny pause added, 'I've been thinking about that patient we operated on this morning, Mrs Tander. I can't help thinking her injuries were inconsistent with the details we were given about the accident.'

'Have you spoken to the police?'

He drummed his fingers on the table for a moment before he answered. 'Not yet. But I'm considering it. I don't want to create suspicion unnecessarily—it would cause a lot of distress to the family. But the husband escaped with minor bruising—strange, considering he was the driver. That sort of head injury can be caused by hitting the steering-wheel if airbags aren't fitted or didn't inflate.'

'Her side hit the tree,' Georgie pointed out. 'It's not unreasonable that she would take the brunt of the impact.'

'I know, but I have a gut feeling about this.'

She raised her brows at him. 'You're starting to sound like Rhiannon,' she told him. 'She's into feeling and intuition and other things heading towards the paranormal. She even consults a clairvoyant regularly.'

'No kidding?' he said with a crooked smile as he casually hooked one arm over the back of the vacant chair beside him.

Georgie had to tear her eyes away from the bunching of his biceps. 'Yes, her name is Madame Celestia,' she said trying not to stare at the sexy tilt of his mouth. 'Rhiannon is totally convinced the woman has special powers. She even had the gall to consult this woman on my behalf. I would have been really angry if I believed for a minute any of it was true.'

'What did this clairvoyant say about you?' he asked.

'She said I was going to marry a blonde doctor,' she answered with a can-you-believe-it roll of her eyes.

His right shoulder went up and down in a little shrug of assent. 'It could happen.'

She looked at him in surprise. 'You surely don't believe in any of that nonsense, do you?'

'No, of course not, but you are a doctor and spend a large proportion of your time with other medicos so it's not unreasonable to assume you'll end up in a relationship with one at some point. Most of my medical friends are hooked up with colleagues. Besides, who's got the time to go anywhere else to meet someone?'

She gave him an embittered look. 'I've had two relationships with doctors and both of them were disasters. My last one had an ex-girlfriend he was still seeing while he was dating me.'

'Yeah, well, I know that feeling,' he admitted ruefully. 'Leila was seeing someone else on the nights I was on call. It had been going on for a couple of months before I found out about it.'

'That's terrible!' Georgie said. 'You must have been devastated.'

He gave a dismissive shrug. 'I should have known she wasn't the right one. My sister hated her on sight and so did my mother.'

'You're really close to your family, aren't you?' she asked.

His eyes met hers across the table. 'When you've been through the sort of stuff we've been through as a family you either pull together or pull apart. We were lucky enough to pull together. My stepfather is a great man who has been a fabulous father figure to me, even though no one could ever really replace my real father. I have enormous respect for Jack as it's the hardest job in the world to love someone else's kid.'

Georgie felt another tight gear shift in her chest. 'You are lucky as I have several friends who positively loathe their stepparents,' she said. 'It's made their relationships with their real parents very strained, which is terribly sad.'

'As I said, it's not easy taking on the responsibility of

someone else's children, but Jack has done so without complaint,' Ben said. 'In fact, if you hadn't been told you'd never guess I wasn't his biological child. He treats me exactly the same as he treats Hannah.'

'I'm looking forward to meeting her,' Georgie said.

'Thanks for coming to the rescue,' he said. 'I was starting to panic about helping her choose underwear and things like that. There's eighteen years between us so she's always been a little girl to me, but now she's thinking about boys and dating. It's scary stuff.'

'It's hard, being a girl,' she said, 'especially at that age. You're sort of stuck with a foot in both camps. Not quite an adult, not quite a child.'

He picked up his coffee again. 'Was it hard for you, growing up as an only child?'

She ran her finger over the raised logo again. 'I had my moments of wishing I had less of my parents' company but on the whole I think I've been lucky. Although I've often wondered what it would have been like to have a brother or sister, especially now as my parents seem a bit lost and vulnerable.'

'I can't imagine your father ever allowing himself to be vulnerable,' he commented. 'He's the archetypal control freak.'

'Not according to Madeleine Brothers,' she put in with a tilt of her chin. 'She spoke of him with nothing but praise, so your attempt to discredit him in my eyes failed. No one I've spoken to thus far has said a bad word about him.'

'That's because you've been speaking to the wrong people,' he countered. 'Madeleine worked with him for a short time in a private hospital, not a cash-strapped public one with overworked staff.'

'She warned me about you,' Georgie said. 'She said you were a heartbreaker.'

His brows lifted slightly. 'Did she?'

'Yes.'

'I can assure you I am nothing of the sort,' he said. 'For one thing I don't have the time to date indiscriminately, and secondly I'm starting to feel the need to settle down.'

Georgie couldn't help feeling surprised by his open admission. Most men his age were reluctant to date monogamously, one-night stands and short-term casual hook-ups being the preferred choice of dealing with their sexual needs.

'You look as if I've suddenly grown two heads,' he commented. 'Isn't it *de rigueur* for an almost thirty-five-year-old man to admit to wanting a wife and family?'

'It's not all that common these days,' she said. 'Most of the men I've met are commitment-shy. The mere mention of a baby sends them running faster than a greyhound on steroids.'

He smiled at the cynical twist to her mouth. 'You've obviously been meeting the wrong men, Georgie. I know about twenty farmers who are desperately looking for a good woman to settle down with. Perhaps it's just city men who don't want the whole deal.'

She lowered her gaze from the deep blue intensity of his. 'Perhaps…'

'Come on,' he said after a tiny pause. 'We'd better get back to work. You're working on Richard DeBurgh's theatre list with him this afternoon, aren't you?'

'Yes,' Georgie said as she followed him out of the café, her forehead beginning to furrow in a frown of apprehension.

He looked down at her as they waited for the pedestrian lights to change. 'Don't be nervous, Georgie,' he said. 'You're doing just fine.'

She gave him a little lopsided smile. 'Thanks, it's kind of you to say so.'

He led the way as the 'walk' sign appeared, his long strides making her almost skip to keep up. 'We need to get together some time in the next week or so to work on your research proposal,' he said as they went through the front entrance. 'I'm seeing public patients in the clinic this afternoon and I'm operating at Greenfield Private tomorrow, so how about Friday afternoon, say, five?'

'OK,' she said. 'Shall I meet you in your office?'

'Yes, that would be good. I have to pick up Hannah at Central Station at seven so that should give us enough time to get the outline down on paper.'

He reached for his mobile as it started to ring. 'Ben Blackwood,' he said, and frowned as he listened to the caller. 'All right. I'll be there in ten minutes.'

'An emergency?' Georgie asked.

'Not here,' he answered. 'One of my private patients has developed pneumonia. I'd better go and have a look at him before I start my public clinic. If anything comes in while I'm away, get Madeleine to cover for me. I'll give her a call now to warn her.' He opened his phone again and added before he pressed rapid dial, 'Don't forget what I said about my suspicions about Mrs Tander. Gut feelings aside, I haven't heard anything from the police and until I do, let's keep a lid on it.'

'Good idea,' Georgie said and watched as he strode back out of the hospital entrance, the phone pressed to his ear as he chatted to his colleague, his long legs making short work of the distance to where his utility was parked in the hospital car park.

She let out a shaky little sigh and turned towards the lifts. A girl could get kind of used to having that heartbreakingly handsome smile bestowed on her every day of her life.

CHAPTER TEN

GEORGIE was totally exhausted by the time her list with Richard DeBurgh ended and she still had three more hours of on call before she could finally relax. Richard had been encouraging towards her but he was nothing like Ben in Theatre. Richard had a tendency to snap at the nursing staff if instruments weren't handed to him quickly enough, and when a patient with a meningioma had a major venous bleed from the sagittal sinus he swore as his tension level rose, which made everyone feel on edge. At one point he bellowed at Georgie for bumping the microscope while he was suturing the sagittal sinus bleed, and although he had moved it himself, she knew there was no point in trying to defend herself.

Linda Reynolds, the scrub nurse Georgie had met in Ben's theatre on her first day, caught up with her in the female change rooms once the list was over.

'See what I mean about there being a waiting list to work on Ben's lists?' she said as she stripped off her theatre scrubs. 'Richard is fine unless things go awry. Don't take it too personally if he occasionally shouts at you. He's not the first and he probably won't be the last.'

'I know,' Georgie said. 'I hate it when surgeons do that though. It doesn't help things at all to lose your cool. I get so flustered when people shout at me and that's when mistakes get made. Why don't they offer compulsory anger management courses at the college?'

Linda smiled as she untied her bandana. 'Tell me about it,' she said. 'Mind you, your father had a bit of a temper at times.'

Georgie met the scrub nurse's gaze in the mirror. 'I've heard both good and bad reports about my father,' she said. 'It makes me feel a bit confused. He's never raised his voice to me once in the whole of my life. He's one of the most placid people I know.'

Linda bent down to pull off her paper overshoes. 'Yeah, well, stressful jobs have a habit of extracting different facets of personality from all of us, I guess. The angel at home, the devil at work scenario is very common,' she offered. 'Take me, for instance. I'm fanatical about cleanliness in Theatre and yet you should see my kitchen at home. It drives my husband nuts. He's forever coming after me with antibacterial spray and paper wipes when I'm cooking.'

Georgie smiled. 'I guess you're right.'

Linda straightened and turned to look at her directly. 'How are you and Ben getting along after your rough start?' she asked.

Georgie wondered if anyone had seen them have coffee that morning or dinner the night before. The hospital community was a small one and many staff members lived locally. Gossiping about colleagues was an occupational hazard—one she wanted to avoid if she could. 'Fine,' she answered, shifting her gaze. 'He's been very gracious about it all.'

'He's a gorgeous guy and I don't just mean in looks,' Linda said. 'He's got such a heart for patients. I reckon half of the time he spends advocating for patients against ridiculous decisions made by hospital management in their splendid

isolation from the actual people they are meant to listen to.
He works too hard, of course, but, then, most of us around
here do. It's part of the profession, but he always seems to go
that extra mile. I guess it's the country boy in him. You know
what they say—you can take the boy out of the country but
you can't take the country out of the boy.'

Georgie grimaced inwardly at how insulting she had been
when she'd refused his offer of a lift home the previous
evening. She had come across as a toffee-nosed brat, born to
wealth and privilege and overbearingly proud of it.

'Well, I'm off,' Linda said as she went to the door. 'What
are you planning for this evening?'

'Once my on-call is over I'm going to the gym, have some
dinner and then fall into bed.'

Linda's green eyes began to sparkle. 'You sound exactly
like someone else I know,' she said. Patting her tubby belly,
she added, 'Do a couple of hundred abdominal crunches for
me, OK?'

Belinda Bronson was in the cardio room when Georgie arrived,
so she took the treadmill next to her. 'How's it going, Belinda?'
she asked as she started her warm-up. 'Is it your day off?'

'Yep, thank God,' the policewoman said, wiping her
forehead with her wristband. 'I've got four days off. I tell you,
the way I'm feeling after the last few days, if I have to face
another drunken, drugged-up dropout, I'll scream.'

'I don't know how you do it,' Georgie said. 'It must be so
hard dealing with violent people, not to mention being first
on the scene at horrific accidents and murders.'

'You get used to most of it after a while—sometimes unexpected things can get under your guard,' Belinda said. 'My
mother thinks I've toughened up too much. She reckons I
scare men off. But you have to toughen up, don't you? You'd

be the same dealing with sick people. I mean they don't all get better, do they?'

'No, they certainly don't,' Georgie agreed, thinking of Marianne Tander, who was still in a coma and unlikely to recover.

They chatted about other things for a while before Georgie decided to discuss the Tanders' accident with her. She reasoned Belinda was a cop so Ben's instructions to keep things quiet didn't include talking to a member of the police force. She gave Belinda the details of the accident and the injuries the wife had sustained and expressed her own and Ben's concerns that the left-side head injury seemed unusual in a motor vehicle accident unless air bags hadn't been fitted to the car.

'I'll have a look into the accident report for you,' Belinda said. 'It could well have been an old-model car. If there's anything suspicious about it the accident investigation team will get onto it pretty quickly, if they haven't already.'

'Thanks, Belinda,' Georgie said, then looked down at the readout on the treadmill. 'Gosh, I've been running for thirty minutes. It's so much more fun when you've got someone to talk to. An MP3 player isn't the same at all.'

'I saw you talking to a guy last night,' Belinda said. 'I was in the pilates room upstairs. I've seen him in here before. He's totally hot. I wouldn't mind washing his sweaty gym socks, I can tell you.'

Georgie knew she was blushing but hoped Belinda would assume it was from the speed she had selected on the treadmill. 'He's actually my boss,' she confessed.

'Gosh, you lucky thing, you. You should see *my* boss. He's fat, bald as a crystal ball and smokes like a chimney.'

Georgie laughed and reached for her water bottle. 'You could always ask for a transfer,' she said. 'You might get lucky next time.'

Belinda snorted and slowed down the treadmill. 'I'll give you a call when I have some information for you. Have a good night, Georgie.'

Georgie lifted her hand in a wave. 'You, too.'

'What is the meaning of this?' Graham Manning, the CEO, stormed as he thrust a letter in Ben's face on Friday morning. 'If the press gets wind of this we'll never live it down. I want that registrar of yours taken off the training scheme immediately. I don't care whose daughter she is. She's causing an absolute furore, practically accusing Jonathon Tander of attempted murder. He's a high court judge, for God's sake!'

Ben frowned as he scanned the letter from one of Sydney's leading barristers. He hadn't spoken to Georgie since they'd had coffee on Wednesday but it appeared she had made some accusations against the husband of Marianne Tander that the police were now investigating. The husband was threatening to sue and as supervisor of surgical training, Ben was ulti- mately responsible for certifying his registrar's progress and suitability for training.

He looked back at the puce-faced CEO. 'Registrars get taken off training schemes because of their unsuitability for training, Graham,' he said. 'Georgiana Willoughby is one of the best first-year trainees I've seen. I certainly will not suspend her training because of some as yet unsubstan- tiated claim that actually has nothing to do with her capacity for training. I'll discuss this letter with her and get her comments.'

Graham pushed a hand through his thinning hair. 'This could blow up in our faces, Ben. It could be a disaster for the hospital, and my position here. We're trying to maintain a rep- utation as a cutting-edge training hospital. With the budget restraints that have been handed out I'm having to cut services left, right and centre. This could bring litigation on us that could come to millions and we're self-indemnified, which means any payout or legal costs come out of our budget, meaning less money for patient services.'

'I know all that, Graham,' Ben said calmly. 'But this sort of situation is going be increasingly frequent. Mr Tander, QC is obviously upset, and rightly so. His wife is still in a coma and is likely to have significant brain damage if or when she wakes up. Emotions are running pretty high at the moment. I'll have a word with him when I next see him.'

'What's this girl like?' Graham asked. 'I've been told she looks more like a catwalk model than a neurosurgeon.'

'She's just like any other first-year registrar, Graham,' he said. 'A little nervous and lacking experience, but I'm sure in time she'll make a very fine neurosurgeon.'

'I'm not giving any favours to her just because of who her father is,' the CEO insisted. 'She has to prove herself on her own merit, not stand on the shoulders of her old man. And I'm telling you, if this thing blows up in her face, her old man won't be able to save her.'

'This is her first week, for God's sake,' Ben said, struggling to hold back his frustration. 'Besides, she's not the only one who was suspicious about the injuries Mrs Tander sustained. I discussed my own concerns with her when we viewed the CT scans.'

'Oh, ah, I see. So *you're* the one behind this outrageous accusation?' he blustered. With narrowed eyes he went on, 'Or are you taking the rap for her because you're sleeping with her, like everyone around here is already suggesting?'

Ben rose to his feet, his whole body tightening with anger. 'My relationship with Dr Willoughby is not relevant to this discussion. But as it happens, I am not sleeping with her.'

Although I'm seriously tempted, he added silently as he held the CEO's look with steely purpose. 'As far as I'm concerned, she is my current registrar and that's all.'

'Better keep it that way,' Graham said as he stepped towards the door. 'I have a feeling that girl is going to be nothing but trouble.'

Tell me something I don't already know, Ben thought as he sank back to his chair and shoved a hand through his hair.

'Georgie, Mr Blackwood wants to see you in his office—immediately,' Jennifer Patterson informed her once she had finished examining a neck injury from a football game. 'He said he tried your mobile but you didn't answer.'

Georgie grimaced as she looked down at it clipped on the waistband of her skirt. 'Damn,' she said. 'Battery's flat. I was just about to charge it when I was called down here.'

'He sounded pretty uptight,' Jennifer warned her. 'What's going on between you two?'

Georgie stripped off her gloves and carefully avoided Jennifer's gaze. 'Nothing's going on.'

'Are you aware that people around here are speculating on whether or not you're dating him?' Jennifer asked.

Georgie stared at her in wide-eyed alarm. 'Has someone been spying on me or something?'

Jennifer's neat brows lifted. 'So it's true, then. One of the cleaning staff works part time at a gym in Bondi. She said she saw you working out together, looking pretty chummy. She even said you left together.'

'That doesn't mean a thing,' Georgie said. 'We happen to be members of the same gym and work at the same hospital and we live in the same suburb. End of story.'

'He was pretty cut up over his last girlfriend,' Jennifer said. 'She was a hospital physiotherapist. She used to work for the group practice responsible for Ben's post-operative patients. I don't think he's dated anyone since.'

'I'm sorry to hear he had his heart broken but, really, it's nothing to do with me,' Georgie insisted.

Jennifer looked up at the clock on the wall. 'You'd better get down and see what he wants. In the whole time I've worked with him I've never heard him so impatient to see someone.' Her eyes twinkled as she added, 'Maybe he's falling for you, Georgie.'

'I don't think so,' Georgie said, although her stomach felt like a thousand tiny wings were flapping inside her as she made her way to his office.

Ben's office door burst open before she could even raise her hand to knock on it. 'You have a heck of a lot of explaining to do, young lady,' he growled as he practically dragged her into his office and slammed the door behind her. 'I've had the CEO breathing down my neck all morning about Jonathon Tander's threats to sue you, me and the entire hospital. What have you done?'

Georgie blinked at him in shock. 'I—I didn't do anything…'

He scooped a letter off his desk and thrust it into her hands. 'Have a look at this. Maybe this will jog your memory.'

She read the wordy legal document, her stomach folding over in alarm, her throat drying up completely as she returned her worried gaze to his furious one. 'I mentioned what we discussed to a police officer friend of mine. I thought that would be OK as it wasn't like I was talking to just anyone. She said she'd look into the accident report. I had no idea it would go this far. I haven't even heard from her about it. The case must have been handed on to someone else.'

His frown was so heavy his eyebrows were almost

touching. 'I told you not to speak to anyone about this. If you wanted to mention it to this cop friend of yours, you should have discussed that with me first. You had no right to talk casually to a friend about a patient under my care. It's totally unprofessional for a start, not to mention the damage it could do to a high-profile man's reputation. He's a high court judge for pity's sake! He is clearly devoted to his wife. He has barely left her bedside. What do have to say for yourself?'

Georgie could feel herself shrinking under the blaze of his anger. She struggled to keep the tears back, her chin wobbling dangerously and her teeth digging into her bottom lip to stop it from trembling. 'I'm sorry…' she gulped. 'I didn't mean this to happen. I thought it would be all right. I had no idea it would come to this.'

'The CEO has asked me to remove you from the training scheme.'

She brushed at her eyes and swallowed back a sob. 'I'm so sorry…but I understand you have to do what you have to do.'

His gaze meshed with hers. 'Well, I'm not going to do it,' he said after a small silence.

She blinked up at him again. 'Y-you're not?'

He scraped a hand through his hair before stuffing both of his hands in his trouser pockets. 'No, because I had the very same concerns about Marianne Tander myself. It hardly seems fair to dismiss you for what could well turn out to be a real case of attempted murder.'

'But you said the husband is devoted to her,' she said, quickly disguising a little watery sniff.

'I know. But that doesn't mean it couldn't all be an act.'

'I don't know what to say…' She twisted her hands in front of her. 'I feel so stupid. Belinda is a friend from the gym. She was at the accident with little Jasmine, you know…the baby with the heart defect? I trusted her to be discreet in her enquiries. I didn't for a moment think it would go any further than a covert look at the record of the accident. The investigating officer must have mentioned my name in the report...'

Ben let out a sigh and, taking his hands out of his pockets, touched her on the shoulder with one of his hands. 'It's all right, Georgie,' he said reassuringly. 'We'll no doubt have to weather a storm for the next few days, but I'm not going to remove you from the training scheme for at least three reasons. Firstly, I couldn't bear the fallout from your father, secondly, you're proving to be a darn good trainee.'

She moistened her lips with the tip of her tongue, her eyes still locked on the dark blue depths of his. 'You mentioned three things,' she said in a scratchy whisper.

Ben looked down at her mouth, the slight tremble of her glistening lips making his groin instantly swell with desire. He longed to taste her, to see if she was as soft and sweet as she looked. What would it hurt? he wondered. One kiss was hardly an affair. Besides, it had been months since he'd felt a woman's mouth on his. It was surely time to get back into the water, even if it turned out he was swimming with a shark. She certainly didn't look like it with her big brown eyes. She looked tiny and feminine and adorably trusting and vulnerable, as if he held her future in his hands, which to some degree he did.

He felt his upper body tilting towards her, slowly, as if under some invisible entity was pushing him from behind. His mouth was within a breath of hers, her soft breath wafted over his lips, and then the tip of her tongue peeked out again and he was totally lost.

He crushed her mouth beneath his in a kiss that was both hard but tender at the same time, the softness of her lips a perfect bed for the insistent pressure of his. He drove his tongue through her softly parted lips and his lower body leapt in response as her tongue began to dance and play with his. Heat coursed through him, the burning lava-hot need filling him to bursting point as he held her closer to deepen the kiss. She tasted of strawberries and desire, each stroke and glide of his tongue against hers making him realise how in tune their bodies were. It was like nothing he had ever experienced before. He had the normal needs of any full-blooded male and had had his share of fulfilling sexual relationships, but somehow he suspected that with Georgie everything he had experienced in the past was going to pale into insignificance.

One of his hands cupped her face while the other went to the gentle curve of her breast, his palm feeling the tight bud of her nipple pressing into it. Her tongue flicked against his, her soft mouth hot and sweet and her body pressing against his with increasing need.

He sucked and nibbled on her fuller lower lip, the one she had stuck out at him numerous times in a pout, and his skin lifted all over at the thought of driving into her silky warmth. She was unbelievably responsive. Her body seemed to come alive under the brush and stroke of his hands and mouth and it made him wonder if she had experienced desire at this level before.

Her small white teeth nibbled back at his bottom lip, the tugging sensation sending his senses into overdrive. He was going to explode if he didn't call a halt soon. He felt like a teenager who hadn't yet learnt how to control the trigger on his release. He wanted her so badly he could feel his body preparing for it, the ache unbearable as she brushed against him in increasing urgency.

'OK…' he said, finally managing to drag his mouth off hers, his breathing ragged as he put her from him. 'This might be a good time to stop.'

Georgie looked up at him in a combination of bewilderment and shame. 'I'm sorry…I don't know how that happened…'

'It wasn't your fault,' he said, his body still pulsing with need. 'I shouldn't have touched you on the shoulder.' He dragged a hand through his hair again, making it stand on end. 'I guess it's been too long since I touched a woman other than a patient. My mother and sister are right. I need to get out more.'

'It's all right,' she said, trying to breathe evenly while her heart was still jumping all over the place. 'I understand.'

He put the desk between them and sat down heavily. 'I wouldn't want you to get the wrong idea,' he said. 'That was a momentary lapse and it won't be repeated.'

'I understand,' she said again. Shifting from foot to foot in a nervous schoolgirl manner, she asked, 'Um…do you want to discuss my research project now or shall I come back some other time?'

Ben ran a hand over the rough shadow peppering his jaw. He wasn't sure he had the self-control necessary to get through an hour of planning out a research proposal with her, locked away in his office. The only thing he wanted to research was her body, and the only thing he wanted to propose was a red-hot affair. 'I'll organise another time early next week,' he said. 'I have some paperwork to see to that's urgent.'

She shifted her feet again. 'Can I go now?'

'Yes,' he said. 'I'll see you tomorrow morning, if you haven't changed your mind about helping me with Hannah.'

Her tongue came out and did a nervous little flick over her lips. 'I haven't changed my mind.'

'Right, then,' he said, pulling his eyes away from her mouth. 'If you have any problems with the press, call me. Don't say a thing to anyone other than me. OK?'

'Yes.'

He held her gaze for a fraction longer than necessary. 'I could have happened to anyone, Georgie,' he said. 'Don' blame yourself.'

Georgie wasn't sure what he was referring to, the kiss or the letter from Jonathon Tander's barrister. She didn't stop to find out. She gave him a wobbly smile and left before she was tempted to reach over the desk and pull his mouth back to hers.

CHAPTER ELEVEN

BELINDA BRONSON was coming out of the gym on Friday evening as Georgie was going in. 'Just the person I wanted to see,' she said, pulling Georgie to one side away from the cluster of members near the front door.

'I was going to say the very same thing to you,' Georgie said with a little frown. 'I got into heaps of trouble over talking to you about the Tanders' accident.'

Belinda's expression turned cynical. 'That kind of figures,' she said. 'I spoke to a mate of mine in Traffic—he must have pressed a few too many sensitive buttons. He told me Mr Tander is a legal eagle. Lawyers always think they're above suspicion and that the legal system they represent and defend so volubly in court doesn't apply to them outside it.'

'Yeah, well, he's not just any old legal eagle,' Georgie said. 'He's a high court judge. If he's serious about going ahead with this, my career is over.'

Belinda tapped her top lip for a moment. 'You know, it might be worth having a deeper look into this,' she said. 'Off the record, if you know what I mean.'

'I don't want any more trouble,' Georgie insisted. 'My boss bawled me out this afternoon over it.' *He also kissed me senseless, and I still can't think straight as a result.* 'It's hard enough handling him without this sort of complication to make things worse.'

'As far as I recall from what Ewan McGuire in Traffic told me, Mr Tander was driving a Mercedes. I can't think of the model number offhand, but I do know it had air bags and they were activated on both the driver and front passenger sides.'

Georgie's eyes went wide. 'Really?'

'Yes, but apparently Mrs Tander wasn't wearing a seat belt. The tree had a branch right at the point of impact, the windscreen was smashed and the air bag got punctured as well.'

'I guess that more or less accounts for the severity of the injury, then,' Georgie said with a musing frown.

Belinda nodded. 'Also, Mr Tander was all clear as far as drinks and drugs are concerned,' she said. 'In fact, he's got a squeaky-clean driving record, not bad for nearly forty years of driving.'

'What was the cause of the accident?' Georgie asked. 'Did your friend find out?'

'Mr Tander said a car swerved to his side of the road and he took evasive action and by doing so lost control of his own car and hit the tree,' Belinda said. 'Of course, there were no witnesses and he couldn't recall the make or model of the other car so it's not going to be easy to prove him wrong if he is, in fact, lying. The accident investigation guys are checking out tyre marks on the road—you know, to see if there are any skid marks to verify what Mr Tander said happened—although, if it was wet, which apparently it was in that suburb the morning of the accident, there won't be any skid marks. It could be a few days before the results come in.'

Georgie nibbled at her bottom lip in agitation. 'I wish I'd never mentioned it now,' she said. 'It's probably just one of those out-of-the-blue accidents that no one has any control over.'

'Doesn't hurt to check these things out,' Belinda reassured her. 'Have you met the husband?'

'Not officially but I've seen him by his wife's bed in ICU when I've been passing through,' Georgie answered. 'My boss told me he's a very devoted husband and very upset about his wife's serious condition.'

Belinda gave another cynical twist to her mouth. 'It might be an idea to look at his wife's life insurance policy. It's amazing how devoted husbands can be when several thousand dollars are going to fall into their laps on the death of their partners.'

'You're not going to do that, are you?' Georgie asked with a worried look.

'I'll be very discreet,' Belinda said. 'What's the wife's condition? Is she likely to recover fully?'

'Her head injury was pretty severe,' Georgie said. 'It's likely if she does wake up from the coma she's in, there will be some sort of permanent brain damage.'

Belinda grimaced. 'Sad all round, isn't it? I had a mate in Special Operations who fell from a building on a stake-out. He's not the same person—he doesn't even know who his wife and kids are now. He sits in a wheelchair in a care facility, staring into space.' She blew out a world-weary sigh and added, 'It totally sucks, what life dishes up sometimes.'

'Tell me about it,' Georgie said with another little frown. 'Sometimes I wonder if I'm doing the right thing, pursuing a career in neurosurgery. There aren't always happy endings. Maybe I should have been a dermatologist after all.'

'And stare at ghastly pimples and weeping eczema all day? No way,' Belinda said with a grin. 'Get on with you, Georgie. Neurosurgery is in your blood. You'll be fine once you get over this rough patch. Don't worry about Mr Tander's threats. We'll sort it out our end and see if we come up with anything. But my bet is he's just upset about his role in injuring his wife and is looking for a scapegoat. I've seen it so many times. He probably blames himself for not checking his wife was wearing her seat belt. The guilt he would be feeling would be overwhelming. He'll let it go as soon as he comes to terms with how things are.'

'I hope you're right,' Georgie said. 'I would hate anything else to go wrong in my life. I'm starting to think someone's put a curse on me or something.'

'You don't believe in curses, do you?'

'No, of course not, but ever since I started at Sydney Met my life has spun out of control.'

Belinda winked at her as she hitched her gym bag back on her shoulder. 'That wouldn't have anything to do with that seriously gorgeous boss of yours, would it?'

Georgie tried to roll her eyes but she could see Belinda wasn't buying it. 'He's gorgeous but still getting over a bad break-up,' she said. 'The very last thing I need is another man in my life who isn't over his last love. I hate playing second fiddle. It's so ego-crushing to realise you're not the one he really wants.'

'Has he made a move on you?'

Georgie could feel her colour rising. 'Sort of…'

Belinda's brows lifted expressively. 'Gosh, he's quick off the mark, isn't he? You've only been working there—what is it?—five days?'

'Don't remind me,' Georgie groaned. 'I have the rest of the year to get through and I'm in over my head as it is.'

Belinda gave her a probing look. 'You mean you're a little bit attracted to him?'

'I'm a *big bit* attracted to him,' Georgie confessed. 'He's he sort of guy who says "Love you" to his mum, *and* he adores his kid sister *and* he wants nothing more than to settle down and have a brood of kids. How rare is that these days?'

'Uh-oh,' Belinda said, her expression turning serious. 'He sounds like the dream guy. If I were you I'd be going for it, boss or no boss.'

Georgie whooshed out a sigh. 'I'm going to do an hour on the cross-trainer to stop myself from thinking about him.'

'I hate to remind you, honey, but there's a twenty-minute time limit on the cross-trainers at this time of the evening,' Belinda said.

'Then I'll have to jump machines until he's exercised out of my brain,' Georgie said.

'Don't you mean exorcised?' Belinda asked with a twinkling smile.

Georgie rolled her eyes. 'Don't *you* start,' she said, and, pushing open the door, headed into the change rooms.

'Can you see her yet?' Hannah asked Ben as she peered up and down Market Street. 'What does she look like?'

Ben scanned the bustling January sales crowd for a sun-kissed brown head but so far he couldn't see any sign of her. 'She's about this tall,' he said, holding his hand against his pectoral muscles, 'and she's got blonde highlights in her brown hair. I'm not sure but I think they're natural.'

Hannah looked up at him impishly. 'And what colour eyes does she have?'

He gave her a frown. 'What's with all these questions? She's just my registrar, nothing else.'

'I hope they're not ice-blue, like you know who's were,' she said with a cheeky grin.

Ben shifted his eyes to search the crowd again. 'No, they're not,' he said somewhat absently as he saw a slim figure weaving her way through the crowd on the George and Market Street intersection, the brilliant white slash of her apologetic smile as she bumped into someone seeming to light up the entire street. 'They're the colour of caramel…or toffee…a soft brown…'

'Uh-oh,' Hannah said, as she saw who her brother was zeroing in on.

Ben opened his mouth to say something in return but closed it as soon as a flowery perfume invaded his nostrils.

'I'm so sorry I'm late,' Georgie rushed up to them, her unfettered hair blowing across her face in the hot breeze.

'Not another accident, Dr Willoughby?' Ben asked with an inscrutable look.

'No,' she said, tucking her hair behind her ear. She turned to the petite dark-haired figure beside Ben and put out her hand. 'Hi, you must be Hannah. I'm Georgie.'

'Pleased to meet you, Georgie,' Hannah said with a friendly smile. 'Ben's told me all about you.'

'Oh, dear,' Georgie said, flicking him a quick reproving glance. 'I hope you won't hold it against me.'

Hannah's eyes were dancing as she looked between her brother and his new registrar. 'Of course not,' she said. 'Anyway, you're a whole lot nicer than his last girlfriend. She was—'

'Hannah!' Ben warned.

Hannah gave him a guileless look. 'What?'

'Georgie doesn't want to hear about my private life,' he said. 'Besides, I need a caffeine hit. I hardly slept last night.'

'Were you called in?' Georgie asked as she walked alongside him with his sister on the other.

'Er…no,' he said. 'Hannah was snoring.'

Hannah swung around in mock affront and jabbed him playfully in the chest. 'I was not! You were the one keeping *me* awake.'

'Don't tell me you snore, Mr Blackwood?' Georgie said with a mischievous glint in her eyes.

He gave her a glowering look from beneath his dark brows. 'I haven't had any complaints in the past,' he said.

'He talks in his sleep,' Hannah piped up authoritatively. 'He's done it since he was a little kid. Mum told me.'

'Shut up or I won't buy you those outrageously expensive running shoes you wanted,' he said with a laugh, feigning outrage. 'I'll make you go home and do your homework instead.'

Hannah leaned around the front of her brother to speak to Georgie. 'He doesn't mean it,' she said. 'He's always teasing me.'

Georgie couldn't help smiling at the playful interchange between older brother and much younger sister. She could see the deep affection they had for each other, the banter and mock glares not able to hide the rock-solid relationship they shared.

Hannah now had her arm tucked through his and was beaming up at him adoringly. His dark blue eyes were soft and a half-smile was playing at the edges of his mouth as he looked down at her.

Georgie felt her stomach tilt sideways at the thought of having him look at her with such love shining in his eyes. He was certainly attracted to her if that kiss was anything to go on but, then, it had obviously been a while since he'd played the field so perhaps she was a convenient diversion. Maybe even the fact that she'd said she was in a no-dating phase had made her all the more alluring to him: a case of wanting what he couldn't have. She even wondered if that was why she couldn't stop thinking about him—because he was technically off limits.

'Is here OK?' Ben asked.

'Sorry?' Georgie blinked up at him vacantly. 'What did you say?'

His gaze dipped to her mouth, watching as her tongue flicked over the soft shiny lips, removing a fine trace of lip-gloss. He felt the sudden hard kick of desire deep and low in his belly again and wondered if he had been in his right mind to accept her offer of accompanying him and his sister. How on earth was he going to keep his hands off her? She was temptation from the top of her silky hair to her fuchsia-pink painted toenails peeking out from the high-heeled sandals she was wearing with her sexily tight jeans. Her close-fitting pink top had a scooped neckline which showed a hint of her luscious cleavage, and there was a red cherry emblem just above her right breast, which kept drawing his gaze like a powerful magnet.

Hannah gave him a nudge with her elbow. 'What is it with you guys?' she asked.

'What?' Ben and Georgie said in unison.

Hannah put her hands on her hips in schoolmistress fashion. 'Now, sit down, both of you, and behave yourselves,' she said. 'We're here to have a coffee and there's to be no playing legs and toes under the table either.'

'Surely you don't think—' Georgie began hastily, but she was cut off by Ben's deep voice coming over the top of her lighter one.

'Cool it, Hannah. You're embarrassing Georgie. She's not interested in me any more than I am her. Besides, she's having a bet with a friend that could lose her a thousand bucks if she goes on a date with a man before Easter,' he said. 'Think of how many pairs of shoes you could buy with a thousand big ones.'

'Not all that many,' his sister put in with a little mock pout.

Georgie stared at the beverage menu, hoping her colour wasn't as high as it was feeling from the inside.

Thankfully the waiter approached and took their orders for

coffee. She couldn't help noticing how protective Ben was of his sister when the young male waiter gave Hannah a second look of male appraisal. Ben shuffled his chair a little closer and draped an arm over the back of his sister's chair.

'Don't even think about it, kiddo,' he said when the waiter had moved on. 'You're practically still jailbait and he's not tall enough for you anyway.'

Hannah gave him a little shove. 'That's a horrible thing to say. He can't help it if he's not very tall. Besides, he looks like a film star.'

He grinned at her and ruffled her hair. 'Hollywood stars are OK but you're too young.'

She screwed up her face at him before turning to Georgie. 'Do you have an annoying big brother who screens all your potential boyfriends for you?' she asked.

Georgie smiled. 'No, I don't, but I'm thinking I might have missed out on something pretty special.'

'You haven't,' Hannah said, but her smile belied her tone. She leaned forward with her chin propped by her hands and asked, 'So what is it you look for in a boyfriend?'

Georgie blinked once or twice. 'Um…'

'Hannah, *please*,' Ben said, rolling his eyes.

She slapped him on the arm and, turning back, tilted her head and fixed her expectant gaze on Georgie. 'You were saying?'

Georgie suppressed a giggle at the look on Ben's face. 'Um…let me see now…' She twirled a strand of her hair around her finger in an idle manner. 'A sense of humour is very important,' she said. 'And I hate to sound prejudiced against short men, but I like a man I can look up to, not just in height but in intellect as well.'

'So far so good,' Hannah said with a cheeky smile in her brother's direction.

'And…' Georgie tapped her lips with the tip of her index

finger for a moment. 'I like a man who's not afraid of being in the wrong occasionally.'

'Uh-oh,' Hannah said.

Ben swung his gaze his sister's way and frowned. *'Uh-oh? What do you mean, "Uh oh"?'*

She gave him a surely-you-know-what-I'm-talking-about look. 'Come on, Ben,' she said. 'You hate apologising. It's your one bad point. You're too proud to admit when you've made a mistake.'

'That's complete and utter rubbish.'

'What about Leila, huh?' she said with a pointed look. 'You knew she was all wrong for you the moment you got involved with her, but you wouldn't admit it. Mum and I told you it was going to end in tears, and it did.'

'Yeah, well, not with mine, it didn't,' he growled.

Hannah exchanged looks with Georgie. 'He's lying,' she said. 'He was depressed for months. We were so worried about him we—'

'That's it,' Ben said, getting to his feet. 'I'm not going to sit here listening to you rabbit on about me as if I'm some sort of broken-hearted loser who doesn't know how to pull a decent date. For God's sake, Hannah, no wonder Mum was worried about you being let loose in the city. You're out of control.'

Hannah pouted at him. 'It's true, Ben,' she said. 'You've been moping about for months. It's time to put it behind you.'

An incoming call on Ben's phone caused a momentary diversion. He strode out of the hearing of the other café patrons and Georgie watched him frown and speak in turn. He came back to the table but didn't sit down. 'I'm sorry but I have to leave you to it for a while,' he said. 'I've got a private patient who needs an urgent consultation.'

He turned to Georgie and asked, 'Would you mind hanging

around with my sister for an hour or so? I'll call you when I'm finished.'

Georgie gave him a wide smile. 'I can think of nothing better.'

Ben clipped his phone back on his belt and strode away. *I just knew she was going to say that,* he thought as he headed to where his car was parked.

CHAPTER TWELVE

BEN had seen Emma Stanley's MRI scans two weeks ago but there had been considerable change in her condition since then. The young sixteen-year-old track and field star had a tumour on her lumbar spine, which thankfully was benign, but that didn't mean she was out of the woods by any means. The tumour was pressing against the cauda equina, causing numbness in her buttocks and weakness in her legs.

Surgery was the only option but there were huge risks involved, especially as imaging had shown the tumour was extensive and its removal had the potential to cause damage to multiple nerve roots. She had fallen several times over the last few days and her parents had panicked and contacted him directly rather than wait until Monday to see him in his public clinic, as he had advised them to do.

Ben sat Emma and her parents down in his office. Taking his own chair, he began to run through the risks. 'I know we've talked through all this before but as Emma's symptoms have worsened it won't hurt to go over them again,' he said. 'The tumour is growing rapidly—far more rapidly than I expected. So it's important we get in there and remove it to minimise the risk of permanent damage to the spinal nerves.'

Glenda and James Stanley each gripped one of their wide-eyed daughter's hands. 'We understand, Mr Blackwood,' the father said. 'We just want her to get well and be able to run again.'

Here comes the difficult part, Ben thought as he mentally prepared himself. 'Surgery of any sort has risks,' he began, 'even routine operations. We have to go into surgery understanding what these are.'

'We don't want to frighten Emma, Mr Blackwood. Is it absolutely necessary to go through these in front of her now?' Emma's father spoke with emotion.

'It's hard, I know,' Ben said, before shifting to speak primarily to Emma. 'Emma, you have to have a basic understanding of the potential problems we face, and you have to ask me any questions about specific concerns you as an individual might have, things that might not be such a concern to, say, non-sportspeople.'

'I understand, Mr Blackwood, and I want to know everything,' the young girl insisted. 'It's all right, Dad, Mum,' she addressed her parents. 'I need to know what's ahead of me.'

'So, the risks…' Ben began once the parents had both nodded their agreement. 'We divide them into two groups. First are risks that could occur with any operation—such as infection, bleeding, clots in the legs. For someone of your age and fitness, Emma, these risks are going to be very small.'

'That's good, Mr Blackwood,' Emma said. 'See, Mum? He said the risks are small.' She turned back to Ben. 'So I should be OK, right?'

'We all hope so, Emma. But there's a second category of risks—risks specific to a particular operation. This is where I really want everyone to understand what the possibilities are here,' Ben explained. 'Emma, your tumour is fairly big, and many of the spinal nerves coming off the last few centimetres of the spinal cord look as though they are trapped in the tumour. In order to get rid of every bit of the tumour so it won't come back, I am going to have to peel each nerve root off the tumour. It is possible that some of the nerve roots might be damaged, possibly permanently.'

'What would that mean, Mr Blackwood?' Emma asked, with a worried glance at her parents.

'It would depend which nerve root was damaged,' Ben said. 'The least might be a patch of numbness or weakness. The worst could be those, plus loss of control of bowels and bladder.'

It was Emma's mother who spoke this time. 'Do what you have to do, Mr Blackwood,' she urged. 'She's suffered enough. We just want her to be without pain.'

But what about without mobility? Ben thought as he looked into that concerned maternal gaze that so reminded him of his mother's when Hannah's life had hung in the balance all those years ago. The same haunted shadows were in Glenda Stanley's eyes and those of her husband's. How could he possibly prepare them adequately for what was ahead?

He pulled himself into line with an effort and continued, addressing just Emma this time. 'Emma, we have a huge task in front of us but I'm thinking that with your experience at track and field training you're no slouch when it comes to hard work. Am I right?'

Emma smiled a tentative smile. 'Yep,' she said. 'I like a challenge.'

'Good, because that's what this is going to be,' he said, 'and quite possibly the biggest challenge of your life so far. I can't promise you miracles, you're old enough to understand that, but I can promise you I will do my best to remove that tumour and relieve the pressure on your spinal nerves, but you need to be aware of the risks.'

'Go on,' Emma said, when he paused momentarily.

Ben glanced at the parents, who were now leaning forward slightly in their chairs. His heart contracted in pain for them.

No parent wanted to watch their child's dreams be snatched away from them but he had a responsibility to inform them of the possible outcomes of such invasive surgery. He took a deep breath and sat forward in his own chair, his forearms leaning on the desk. 'I cannot promise you a hundred per cent return to full function,' he said. 'Emma's nerves may already be permanently damaged.'

'You mean…?' It was Glenda who spoke but Ben could see that both Emma and her father knew exactly what she was referring to.

'Yes,' he said heavily. 'There's a chance Emma will never walk again.'

The silence was so heavy he could have reached out and touched it. He waited for the fallout. It always happened. It usually took about five to ten seconds.

One.

Two.

Three.

Four.

'B-but I'm an athlete…' Emma's thin voice cracked the silence. 'Running is my life. I've got sponsors queuing up.'

Ben ached for her. She was the same age as Hannah. He knew all about teenage passion and how focussed they could be on one thing and one thing only, be it boyfriends or fashion or sport. 'I know, Emma,' he said gently. 'I will do the best I can, but you need to know the risks. You have a rare condition. You did nothing to cause it—it's just there and has to be taken care of. That's my job. Your job is to trust me to do what I can to give you a good outcome, but as I said there are no guarantees.'

He waited for a moment to add, 'I always advise patients to get a second opinion in cases such as these. It doesn't reflect on my judgement so, please, don't think I would be in

the least offended by you seeking someone else's opinion. In
fact, I would prefer it.'

'No,' the father said after exchanging another quick glance
with his wife and daughter. 'We've heard you are the best and
we want you to look after Emma. You were the one who di-
agnosed the tumour in the first place after she'd been shuffled
from doctor to doctor for months.'

Precious, precious months, Ben thought with anguish as
he opened his drawer for the necessary consent and admission forms. God, there were times when he really hated his
job.

'So what do you think of my big brother?' Hannah asked as
they finished their coffee. 'Isn't he gorgeous?'

'Er…yes…' Georgie said. 'But I don't want you to think
that there's anything going—'

'A thousand bucks, huh?' Hannah cut her off musingly.
'Don't you think he's worth the payout of your bet?'

Very definitely, Georgie thought, but she wasn't going to
admit it to Ben's sister. She was only starting to admit to
herself that the attraction she felt for him was moving fast
beyond the physical.

Hannah didn't wait for an answer and plunged in again. 'He
got terribly hurt by Leila Ingram. She was sleeping around
behind his back. I was glad when they broke up because I
never liked her in the first place, but I feel bad for him as he's
not dated since. He's nearly thirty-five. He should be married
with a baby on the way by now. I'm dying for a niece or
nephew and Mum and Dad would love a bunch of grandkids.'

Georgie blinked at her helplessly, not sure she was
supposed to contribute to the conversation or simply be a
sounding-board. In the end Hannah took the matter out of her
hands and rattled on some more.

'I'm not sure if you know this but my dad is not Ben's real father. His dad died when he was six in a tractor accident.' She gave a little shudder and continued, 'I still can't look at the bank of that dam without thinking of how dreadful it must have been for Ben to have his father ruffle his hair at breakfast that morning, only to be killed half an hour later.'

Georgie swallowed a thick lump of empathy in her throat for what Ben and his mother had been through. Life was so fragile sometimes—she saw it all the time at work. It was one of the things that challenged her and frustrated her at the same time. Fate laid a heavy hand on some people and a lighter one on others.

'My dad was the owner of the neighbouring property,' Hannah went on. 'He had secretly loved my mum for years. He helped Mum get back on her feet; he did all the farm labour and helped pay for feed, just like Ben is doing now, on account of the drought. My parents would have lost the farm without his help.'

Georgie recalled the pile of invoices she'd seen in his utility that night after the gym and grimaced again at how rude she had been towards him. 'Your brother is a very nice man,' she said. 'It's no wonder you adore him.'

Hannah grinned. 'So you like him a little bit, then, do you?' she asked.

'He's my boss, Hannah,' she said, more to remind herself more than the young girl. 'We have to work together for the next twelve months. Things can get tricky when workplace romances run off the rails. We have to deal with life-and-death situations—there's no room for ill feeling and resentment as it could compromise patient care.'

'Well, I think *he* likes *you*,' Hannah said with sisterly authority. 'He keeps looking at you all the time. Haven't you noticed?'

Georgie was beginning to think Ben's kid sister was a little too observant. If Hannah had already perceived Ben's interest what on earth was she making of *her* pathetic attempt to disguise hers? 'Um...sort of,' she said at last. 'But it's just because we got off to a bad start. Did he tell you what I did to him?'

'No,' Hannah said, leaning forward. 'Tell me what happened.'

Georgie told her the details of that fateful morning, watching as the young teenager's blue-green eyes went wide at first, and then her face falling as reality began to sink home.

'No wonder he didn't tell me or Mum,' Hannah said, nibbling her bottom lip. 'He might have been killed.'

'I'm so sorry. I feel so bad about it. I'm normally so careful but I was nervous about my first day at the hospital...'

A frown was still wrinkling Hannah's forehead. 'I had a terrible accident on my bike when I was seven,' she said in a subdued tone. 'I nearly died. I had to be resuscitated three times on the way to hospital in the ambulance. We don't talk about it much at home. It upsets everyone too much.'

'I'm sorry.'

'It's why Ben chose to do neurosurgery,' Hannah continued. 'He hadn't long qualified as a doctor when I was hit by a car on the road leading to our property. When I came out of a three-week coma with all my faculties working normally, he decided to specialise in neurosurgery.'

'There are lots of patients who are very glad he did,' Georgie put in.

'Yes, I know,' Hannah said. 'So I guess you could say something good came out of something bad. I nearly lost my life but it gave the world a wonderful neurosurgeon as a result.'

'Do you remember anything about the accident?' Georgie asked.

'No, and to tell you the truth I'm kind of glad,' Hannah said. 'All I know is they never caught the driver.'

'Does that make it harder for you?'

'No, not really,' Hannah replied. 'What's the point in being bitter? I have a shunt in my head and a few titanium screws but, hey, I'm alive. I kind of figure the person who knocked me down has suffered more in the long run. Every day he or she has to live with the fact they were too cowardly to stop and help. I couldn't live with myself if it was me.'

Georgie captured her lip again. 'No, neither could I.'

'I'm sure Ben won't hold it against you,' Hannah said at Georgie's worried frown. 'He's not the sort to hold a grudge.'

'Except when it comes to my father,' Georgie said with a rueful twist to her mouth.

'Your father?' Hannah looked at her blankly. 'What's your father got to do with any of this?'

Georgie blew out a little sigh. 'I'm Professor Willoughby's daughter. I'm sure Ben's told you about *him*.'

'Oh, *that* Professor Willoughby,' Hannah said. 'I've only seen Ben truly angry twice in my life. The first time was when I woke up from the coma. He threatened to tear limb from limb the person who had run me down, and the second was when he failed his fellowship. He'd worked three jobs to get himself through medical school. He was doing extra shifts prior to the exam to pay off the rest of the debt, so it was a bit of a blow when he failed. He hadn't had a holiday or even a night off in years. He was so ready to toss it all in but somehow he pulled himself back into line and went for it with even more determination. But, hey, success is the best revenge, right?'

'I guess so,' Georgie said, frowning slightly.

No wonder Ben had been a bit prickly over dinner the other night, she thought. Her life couldn't have been more different from his. She had been brought up with designer clothing; her very expensive education and holidays had been paid for without lifting a single one of her fingers.

Ben, on the other hand, had lost his father at a young age and had had to grow up rather quickly as a result, taking on more and more responsibility for his family. It would have been a truly devastating blow to fail his fellowship but she couldn't for the life of her agree with him that her father had done it out of spite or prejudice.

The waiter came over to collect their empty cups which gave Georgie an opportunity to divert her conversation with Hannah to safer ground. She reached for her bag and slipped it over one shoulder as she got to her feet. 'We'd better get a move on,' she said with a smile. 'What would you like to look at first?'

Hannah was delightful company, Georgie decided an hour or so later when they had both tried on shoes and separates in various boutiques. She talked about her life on the farm and how she wanted to become a kindergarten teacher once she left school. She also talked almost constantly about her big brother, making it even harder for Georgie to control her snowballing feelings towards him.

He wasn't shallow and selfish, like most of the men she had dated in the past, and his core values resonated with her in a way no one else's had done before. He was dedicated and treated his patients as if they were important, not just names on a waiting list. He was devoted to his family and his colleagues adored him. What was not to like about him?

'Do you think my bottom looks big in these jeans?' Hannah asked her at one point, swivelling her head around to check out her rear in the change-room mirror.

'You look fantastic in them,' Georgie said. 'And I think that top we bought earlier will go with them beautifully.'

Hannah put her hands on her on hips and tilted her head from side to side as she looked at her reflection. 'I wish I was a bit taller,' she said. 'It's not fair that Ben's six foot four and a half and I'm only five two. He could have spared a couple of inches for me, don't you think?'

'I know what you mean,' Georgie commented wryly as she hitched up the legs of her jeans to show Hannah the height of her heels. 'I'm probably doing irreparable damage to my ankles and knees in an attempt to look him in the eye occasionally.'

Hannah's eyes twinkled. 'As long as you can reach his mouth to kiss him, that's the main thing.'

Georgie had no way of hiding the red-hot flush that stole over her features.

'Oh, my God!' Hannah crowed. 'You've already done it! I *knew* it! Wait till I tell Mum. She'll be over the moon.'

'Hannah, *please…*'

'There's no point in denying it,' Hannah said, as she unzipped the jeans and busied herself with getting back into her old ones. 'I could see it the moment I saw you together. It's kismet or destiny or something. What's your star sign?'

Georgie mentally rolled her eyes. 'It's not my birthday for months.'

'That reminds me,' Hannah said turning to face her. 'It's Ben's birthday in a couple of weeks. I've already got something in my bag that I made for him especially, but I'd like to get him some new aftershave. Want to help me choose it?'

What could she say? Georgie thought as she was dragged by the hand out of the boutique a short time later and led to the nearest department store.

Hannah was like her brother—totally irresistible.

CHAPTER THIRTEEN

BEN called Hannah on her mobile to arrange a meeting place and half an hour later caught sight of her and Georgie sitting on the grass near the Hyde Park fountain, a pair of ibis coming closer and closer for the crumbs Georgie was tempting them with.

'Even the animal kingdom isn't safe from her natural beauty and charm,' he muttered under his breath as he made his way towards them.

'Hi, Ben, look what I bought,' Hannah said, leaping to her feet and showing him her jeans and top inside the boutique bags she had in her possession.

'Mmm, very nice,' he said. Swinging his gaze to Georgie, who was still sitting cross-legged on the grass, he asked, 'What did you get?'

'Sore feet,' Georgie said wryly, as she made to get up.

He smiled and offered her a hand, pulling her up so strongly she tumbled forward into his arms.

'Ooh!' she said breathlessly, her hands flat against the hard wall of his chest.

'That'll teach you to wear those ridiculously high heels all the time,' he admonished her playfully, his hands sliding down the length of her arms as she found her balance.

'She only does it so she can reach your—'

'*Hannah!*' Georgie gasped, her face exploding with colour.

Ben chuckled as he tugged on his sister's ponytail. 'What have you been up to? Teasing my poor little registrar?'

Hannah just smiled.

The heat of the afternoon lured Ben's little sister away from the shops and off to the beach.

'Why don't you come with us, Georgie?' she asked.

Georgie glanced self-consciously at Ben and began, 'I don't think I—'

'Oh, come on,' Hannah pleaded. 'It will be no fun by myself. Ben will go off surfing for hours and I'll probably drown under the first tiny wave.'

'Don't listen to her, Georgie,' Ben interjected. 'She can swim like a fish and I haven't been on my board since before Christmas, but, please, feel free to join us. It's turning out to be a scorcher and at least you can always head home when you've had enough of us.'

I don't think I could ever have enough of you. Georgie heard that little voice in her head again. 'I was thinking about going for a swim anyway,' she said before she could stop herself. 'I'd be glad of some company.'

A little while later she joined Hannah on the stretched-out beach towels on the sand on Bondi Beach as Ben headed for the rolling waves.

'Can you surf?' Hannah asked as she handed Georgie the sunscreen she'd borrowed from her earlier.

'I've never tried,' she answered. 'I've thought of having lessons but I never seem to find the time.'

'Ben could teach you,' Hannah said. 'Look at him.' She pointed to his tanned, muscular body paddling out to where the waves were forming. 'There he goes. That's not bad for a boy born and bred in the bush, now, is it? Isn't he cool?'

I don't know about cool but he's certainly hot, Georgie thought as she watched him carving his way through and along the wave until it finally crashed. He picked up the board and paddled out strongly again, his rippling muscles glistening and his black hair gleaming in the bright summer sunshine.

'How about a swim?' she asked, hoping to skirt away from the subject of Ben for a while to give her heart rate a chance to settle back to somewhere near normal.

Hannah jumped to her feet. 'Race you to the water!'

Georgie let her win but by only the narrowest margin. The water was refreshingly cool after the heat of the sun and she swam out beyond the breakers, reassured once she had checked that, like Ben had said, his sister could swim very well indeed.

They body-surfed among the other swimmers, which was difficult at times as the section between the flags was crowded, but when Hannah suggested they move outside the patrolled area, Georgie insisted they stay.

'It's not worth it, Hannah,' she said. 'I know you're a great swimmer but the rips can be treacherous at times and there are sometimes sandbars. I saw a patient with a permanent neck injury at my last hospital. He dived under a wave and broke two of his vertebrae on a sandbar. He was supposed to be getting married the following week. His fiancée eventually left him. It was so sad.'

Hannah brushed her wet hair out of her eyes as they waded through the shallows back to their towels. 'How do you cope with all the unhappy endings, Georgie?' she asked. 'Mum is always worrying about Ben and what he has to face each day. I guess because of my accident she is more aware of what the

octors and nurses go through, as well as the patients and their
amilies.'

'It's really hard at times,' Georgie answered with honesty.
'We're trained to maintain a clinical distance but at times certain
patients slip under your guard.' *Not to mention certain doctors!*

'I couldn't do it,' Hannah said as she flopped down on her
owel. 'That's why I want to work with kids. I'm figuring the
most I'll have to deal with is a nosebleed or wet pants.'

'I'm planning on working with kids, too.'

'You mean in paediatrics?'

'Yes,' Georgie said. 'I'm a bit of a soft touch when it comes
o little kids.'

'So you want to have some of your own?'

Georgie poked her painted toenails into the sand. 'Yes, but
want to finish my fellowship first.'

'But that's four years away and Ben will be nearly forty!'
Hannah gasped.

Georgie swung her gaze to Hannah's. 'I'm your brother's
current registrar, not the future mother of his children,' she
said with as much force as she could muster. 'Besides,' she
added for effect, 'I've been told by a clairvoyant I'm going
o marry a blond man.'

Hannah gave her a scathing look. 'You don't believe in all
hat nonsense, do you?'

Georgie hitched up one brow. 'Who was asking me what
my star sign was an hour or so ago?'

Hannah gave her a sheepish smile. 'Sorry, but I really like you
and I want Ben to find someone who won't let him down, like
Leila did. You'd make a fantastic sister-in-law, and think of the
fun we could have, shopping and doing our hair and make-up.'

Georgie smiled back. 'You're a real sweetie, Hannah. But
don't want you to get your hopes up when life might have
other plans.'

A tall shadow blocked out the glare of the sun and some droplets of sea water landed on Georgie's shoulders. She looked up into Ben's dark blue gaze and her stomach did funny little dance-like shuffle that sent aftershocks down her legs to her toes.

'Have you both got sunscreen on?' he asked.

'Yes,' Georgie and Hannah answered in unison.

'Good,' he said. He reached for the bottle and handed it to his sister. 'Can you do my back, Hannah?'

'I'm just off to the loo,' she said, leaping to her feet and thrusting the bottle into Georgie's hands. 'Georgie will do it won't you, Georgie?'

Georgie took the bottle. 'Er…yes…'

'You don't have to if you don't want to,' Ben said when Hannah had scampered off.

'It's fine,' she said with a tight little smile. 'I wouldn't want you to blame me some time in the future for getting a melanoma.'

Ben could hardly concentrate on her words as her soft little hands began to smooth the lotion over his back. He could feel his whole body spring to life under her exquisite touch, the stroke and glide of her hands and fingers making his blood surge away from his brain where he most needed it to remind himself of how dumb it would be to get involved with her. She had only been on the unit a week and the rumours were already flying. And now Hannah was actively encouraging a liaison between them. Sure, it felt good to have his kid sister's instant approval but that didn't mean he had to dive head first into a relationship with the daughter of a man who had done his best to sabotage his career before it had even got off the ground.

He suppressed a sigh of pleasure as her hands skated over his shoulder blades. He wanted her to do his front and not just his chest but lower where he was aching to feel the satin softness of her fingers…

Georgie couldn't believe the way Ben felt under her fingertips. She had been dreaming of doing this, running her hands over him, feeling the hard-muscled smoothness of his skin, sensing the inherent strength and power of him just beneath the surface. She wished she had the courage to push him down on the towel on his back and do his front, lingering over his taut pectoral muscles, circling the indentation of his belly button before going lower where a trail of dark masculine hair disappeared tantalisingly into his board shorts, over a well-formed six-pack.

She had hung around gyms ever since her late teenage years but in all that time she hadn't seen anyone with the spectacular build he had. It wasn't grotesquely overdone, as some male gym junkies aspired to. Instead, it spoke of a man who loved his sport but knew how to maximise its benefits without compromising his health and vigour.

'Do you want me to do yours?' Ben asked into the silence.

'I—I'm fine…'

He took the bottle from her hands and squirted some of the contents out into the palm of his hand. 'Turn around,' he commanded. 'You've been in the water so what you put on earlier would have washed off by now.'

She wriggled away from the temptation of his touch. 'It's waterproof for four hours.'

His eyes clashed with hers. 'You rubbed my back so it's only fair that I rub yours, right?'

Georgie turned around rather than have that blue gaze see too much. 'Um…right…'

She tried to disguise her sucked-in breath as his hands ran over her in long slow movements that sent a shockwave of reaction across the floor of her belly. Her traitorous thoughts started to drift away from her control. How would it be to have his hands on her in other more intimate places? Her body was already tingling with sensations she had never felt before. It was as if he had cast a spell on her or something. He had only to look at her with those dark eyes of his and she felt like rolling over and playing bed.

'Ben! Georgie! Come quickly.' Hannah rushed up to them, her feet kicking sand in all directions in her haste. 'Someone's been injured by a surfboard.'

Ben dropped the bottle of sunscreen and sprang to his feet as he saw the lifeguards bringing in a surfer with blood seeping from a gash on his forehead. As far as he could tell, the young man was unconscious as the lifeguards placed him on the mat under the shade of the surf club tent and rolled him onto his side into the coma position.

Ben quickly informed them he and Georgie were doctors before he took control. 'Georgie, stabilise his neck while I check his airway.'

Georgie placed a hand onto each side of the surfer's head to prevent further neck movements while Ben applied a jaw thrust to open the airway. The lifesavers had opened their resuscitation kit, which included a mask and bag and a small oxygen supply. Ben fitted the mask and turned on the oxygen. Fortunately the patient was breathing spontaneously, and his colour looked good.

'Is there a hard collar in that kit?' Georgie asked.

One of the lifeguards passed her a universal hard collar, which Georgie adjusted to fit the patient and applied to his neck.

Ben donned a pair of gloves and examined the head wound. There was no bony crepitus or palpable fracture, just a large gash in the scalp, which was bleeding profusely. He applied a couple of gauze dressing pads and held them in place while Georgie firmly bandaged the skull to control the bleeding. He then checked the surfer's pulse and blood pressure while Georgie listened to the patient's chest.

'Sounds like he's aspirated some water,' she said.

'We've already called an ambulance,' one of the life-guards said.

'Good,' Ben responded. 'He'll need full A and E assessment.'

He checked the swimmer's pupils, finding them equal and reactive, and did a GCS, assessing it at about 11 or 12. There were no other obvious injuries. The main problem appeared to be the scalp laceration and concussion, as the surfer was now showing signs of regaining consciousness.

'The ambulance is here,' the senior lifeguard informed them.

'W-what happened?' The patient opened his eyes, his expression confused and disoriented. 'What's going on?'

'You'll be fine,' Ben reassured him. 'You hit your head on your board and briefly lost consciousness. We're sending you to hospital for further assessment.'

The still groggy patient was soon bundled into the back of an ambulance, with a hand-written note from Ben, outlining his and Georgie's assessment and treatment.

'I'm not so sure I'll give surfing a go after all,' Georgie said as they made their way back to their towels. 'It looks far too dangerous.'

'I offered her lessons with you,' Hannah explained to Ben.

'Oh…' he said, grimacing slightly.

'You'd be OK with that, wouldn't you?' Hannah asked, looking up at him with appeal.

'Sure.'

'I'm not sure I want to—' Georgie began.

'You'd be great at it, Georgie,' Hannah insisted. 'You're a natural, isn't she, Ben? She's fit and supple and a good swimmer.'

And she's bloody heart-stoppingly gorgeous in that pink and orange bikini, he added mentally. Just how *did* she keep her breasts inside those tiny triangles?

'I'm starving,' Hannah announced. 'Where are we going for dinner?'

'I have to get home,' Georgie said, not wanting to intrude any further.

'Oh, no, you must come with us, mustn't she, Ben?' Hannah asked. Swinging her gaze back to Georgie, she added, 'Ben will only talk about boring work stuff unless you're there.'

'I don't think I should.'

'Save me from her, Georgie,' Ben said with a crooked smile. 'If you don't come, all I'll hear all night is stuff about totally unsuitable boyfriends. It drives me nuts.'

She bit her lip and then released it. 'If you're sure…'

'We're sure,' he and Hannah said in unison.

Georgie just smiled.

'*Dinner?*' Rhiannon looked at Georgie with suspicion. 'That's a date, isn't it?'

'Not when there's a sixteen-year-old chaperone,' she said with a speaking glance. 'His kid sister is coming, too.'

'Yeah, right.' Her flatmate rolled her eyes. 'That's what they all say.'

'It's true,' Georgie said as she inserted a dangly earring into her left ear lobe. 'Her name is Hannah and she's lovely. She talks way too much about her brother, of course, but that's to be expected, I guess, as he's eighteen years older than her and a bit of a hero figure to her.'

'And what about you?' Rhiannon asked with a probing look. 'Is he hero material?'

Georgie sent her eyes heavenwards. 'Sometimes I wonder if I did the right thing in agreeing to this stupid bet. It's like tempting fate to say you won't do something, for all of a sudden the very thing you've sworn not to do is dangled in front of your nose until you can't think straight.'

Rhiannon put out her hand palm upwards. 'Pay up, sister. You're going to have to anyway so why not get it over with?'

Georgie set her shoulders. 'No,' she said. 'After Andrew I said I wouldn't even dip my toes into the dating swamp for three months minimum and I meant it.'

'That was before you met Ben Blackwood,' Rhiannon reminded her.

'I can be strong,' Georgie said as she inserted the other earring. 'I can do this, I know I can. So what if he's good-looking and loves his little sister and keeps his family's farm afloat by paying all the bills for them.'

Rhiannon's eyes bulged. *'He does all that?'*

'Yes, *and* he loves his stepfather.'

'Uh-oh,' Rhiannon said, handing Georgie her lipstick.

Georgie stared at the slim tube for a moment.

'What's wrong?' Rhiannon asked. 'Don't you think it's the right colour? I think it goes brilliantly with your outfit. That dress looks sensational on you by the way. I wish I had your figure. Maybe I'll join the gym after all.'

'I think I'll just wear lip-gloss,' Georgie said with a tiny frown creasing her brow. 'I don't want to overdo it.'

'Believe me, Georgie, you could turn up dressed in a garbage bag and you'd be overdoing it,' Rhiannon said wryly. 'One look into those big brown eyes of yours and he's going to be lost, if he's not already.'

Georgie gave her flat mate a big squishy hug. 'You're so good for my ego,' she said. Putting Rhiannon from her, she asked earnestly, 'You won't be too lonely here all by yourself, will you?'

'I'm not going to be…I mean…er…not at all,' Rhiannon said quickly. 'I've got some work to do on my PhD philosophy paper. I'm going to the university library for a couple of hours.'

'As long as you're sure?'

'Totally.'

Georgie took a deep breath and inspected her ensemble in the full-length mirror. 'Well, then...'

The doorbell rang and Rhiannon handed her the tiny evening purse she'd selected to wear with her cerise dress and high-heeled sandals.

'If you're going to blow a thousand mackeroos, make sure it's worth it,' she said with a cheeky grin.

It will certainly be worth it, Georgie thought as she answered the door.

CHAPTER FOURTEEN

BEN had to force his eyes to stay fixed on Georgie's face as she opened the door at his summons. She was dressed in a knock-out pink dress that skimmed her slight curves and highlighted the healthy glow of her skin. Her hair was loose about her shoulders, its sun-kissed light waves full of body and bounce, making his fingers twitch yet again to reach out and thread through its silkiness. Her perfume drifted towards him, a different one this time. It was a subtle but totally intoxicating scent that reminded him of sun-warmed honeysuckle.

'Hannah is waiting in the car,' he said by way of greeting, not able to think of anything else on the spot. 'She had a good day today. Thank you.'

Georgie followed him towards the lifts. 'I had fun, too,' she said. 'She's a lovely girl and great company.'

He stabbed at the lift button without looking at her. 'I can't help worrying about her,' he confessed with a small frown. 'She's lived in the country all her life. She's not as street smart as city kids.'

'She's fine, Ben,' Georgie reassured him. 'I thought she was very mature for her age.'

He sighed and held the lift doors open with his arm as it

arrived, waiting until she stepped inside before joining her.
'She had to grow up pretty fast,' he said, still frowning. 'She
spent months in rehab, regaining her mobility. I still get nightmares thinking about it, you know…' He paused momentarily. 'What could have happened…'

She couldn't stop herself from reaching out to touch him
on the arm, her fingers curling into the solid warmth of his
flesh. 'It didn't happen, Ben,' she said softly. 'She's fine.'

Ben looked down at the slim fingers curled around his
forearm and, almost without knowing he was doing it, rested
his on top. 'I have a patient the same age as Hannah booked
in for Monday's list,' he said. 'That was who I had to see
earlier today. She's the same age, the same height—she even
looks like her.'

Georgie drew in a tight little breath as she met his haunted
gaze. 'What's wrong with her?' she asked.

'She has cauda equina syndrome, from a nerve sheath
tumour. It's large, and it's wrapped around most of the lum-
bosacral nerve roots. There's a reasonable risk of permanent
damage. She could end up with lower limb weakness or
urinary or faecal incontinence.'

'What do you think the risk is of leaving permanent dys-
function?' she asked.

He sighed again. 'Pretty high I'm afraid. The literature
suggests no better than 50 per cent chance of avoiding nerve-
root compromise.'

Georgie bit her lip. 'That's not good.'

The lift doors opened and, placing his hand on her elbow,
Ben led her outside. 'No,' he said. 'It's at times like these that
I sometimes I wonder if I should have been a dermatologist.'

She looked at him in surprise. 'That's totally weird,' she
said, and gave her head a little shake.

'What's weird?' he asked. 'The thought of being a dermatologist? Think of it—no on-call, no eighty- to ninety-hour weeks and no weekends stuck in Theatre while everyone else is at the beach.'

'I know what you mean,' she said thinking of how much she had enjoyed being in the warm summer sunshine all afternoon. 'But I meant it was weird you said that because I said the very same thing to my policewoman friend the other day.'

'Have you spoken to her since then?' he asked.

She couldn't quite read his expression. 'No.'

He blew out a tiny breath. 'I think I should warn you things might be pretty uncomfortable for you in ICU just now. It might be best to keep your visits to a minimum until this thing with Mr Tander settles down a bit.'

'Has he said anything to you lately?'

Ben decided against telling her of the interaction he'd had with Marianne Tander's husband as he'd been leaving his office after seeing Emma Stanley and her parents that morning. Jonathon Tander had cornered him, demanding to know why he hadn't yet sacked the registrar who had cast such wicked aspersions on his impeccable character. The man's heated tirade had gone on for so long Ben had begun to wonder if Mr Tander was protesting rather too much. Ben understood the volatility of emotions, especially in ICU where lives so often hung in the balance, but something about Jonathon Tander was a little too self-righteous for his liking.

'Not lately,' he lied, as he opened the car door.

'Hi, Georgie,' Hannah said as she wriggled out of the car to make room for her on the bench seat. 'Gosh, you look fabulous, doesn't she, Ben?'

'Er…yeah…she does,' Ben answered, dragging his eyes away from the shadow of Georgie's cleavage as she slid along the seat.

'I love your perfume,' Hannah said, sniffing the air vigorously as she got in beside Georgie. 'It's so subtle, not like the woman's whose name I've been forbidden to mention. *She* smelt like one of those cheap toilet air fresheners,' she pinched her nose and added, '*Eeeuw*.'

Georgie glanced at Ben's expression and saw him frowning darkly as he shifted the car into gear. She hadn't realised until now how terribly hurt a man could be about a break-up. She had assumed they quickly moved on to the next relationship as a couple of her ex-partners had done, but it was clear Ben hadn't really come to terms with Leila's betrayal. It was also very clear his sister was doing her best to match-make them, which was rather sweet, but Georgie had a feeling Hannah's attempt to marry her off to her big brother was likely to fail. He was undoubtedly attracted to her, as she was to him, but their backgrounds were so different and his prejudice against her father would surely cause trouble if their relationship did become a permanent one. She could just imagine the friction it would cause—maintaining a successful relationship was hard enough without other factors coming into play.

'Have you got enough room?' Hannah asked.

'Um…yes…' Georgie answered, trying to ignore the rock-hard thigh brushing against hers. She sucked in a breath to keep her upper body away from his but it was almost impossible as Hannah seemed to be leaning against her, she could only assume deliberately.

'Is Thai food all right with you?' Ben asked into the little silence.

'Of course,' Georgie answered. 'I love Thai food.'

'There's a fabulous Thai restaurant in The Rocks,' he said. 'It's right next to Cadman's cottage.'

'I know the one,' Georgie said. 'It's won numerous awards.'

A short time later they were seated in the busy restaurant, with drinks in front of them, while Hannah monopolised the conversation.

'So when are you going to bring Georgie home to meet Mum and Dad?' she asked her brother. Before waiting for an answer, she tacked on, 'How about next weekend?'

'I really don't think—' Ben and Georgie spoke in unison.

'Why not?' Hannah asked. 'Georgie would love it, wouldn't you, Georgie?'

'Um…I…'

'I bet you'd love to have a ride on one of our horses,' Hannah said. 'And Ben could show you around some of the vineyards in the area.'

'It sounds lovely but—'

'It's not like it's a date or anything,' Hannah said. 'Anyway, it's me inviting you, not Ben, so how about it?'

'It's a lovely offer, Hannah,' Georgie said, 'but I think I'm on call next weekend.'

'What about the one after that?' Hannah asked hopefully.

'I'm sure Georgie has a hectic social life in the city. No doubt a weekend in the country would be far too boring for her,' Ben put in as he examined the menu.

'On the contrary, I can think of nothing better than a weekend in the country,' Georgie said, sending a reproachful look in his direction.

'Well, that's settled, then,' Hannah said dusting her hands as if a particularly difficult mission had just been accomplished. 'The weekend after next it is.'

'Thank you for dinner,' Georgie said later that evening as Ben walked her to the entrance to her apartment while Hannah waited in the car, busily texting a friend on her mobile phone. 'I had a wonderful time.'

He gave her a wry smile. 'Thank you for putting up with my sister's not-too-subtle attempts to find me a wife. I hope you weren't too embarrassed.'

'Not at all,' she said, feeling her cheeks grow warm as his dark blue gaze rested on her face.

The silence began to stretch, second by second, the air starting to crackle with tension as Georgie found her eyes slowly but inexorably drifting towards his mouth. His lips were so tempting she wanted to stand on tiptoe and press her mouth against them, to stroke the tip of her tongue across the seam of his mouth, to push in and find the sexy rasp of his. She felt her heels start to come up off the floor, her body tilting towards him, her eyelashes starting to come down…

The first brush of her mouth against his sent shooting sparks of heat right through Ben's body. He felt it in every limb, vein and artery. His groin leapt to attention, his heart ramming against his chest as his tongue met hers as he took over the kiss.

He had kissed a lot of women in his time but never had he kissed a woman with as much passion as Georgie. She didn't just kiss with her mouth—she kissed with her whole body. He could feel it pressed up against him, her breasts crushed to his chest, her legs between the brace of his, her arms flung around his neck to keep his mouth on hers, her hot, dancing little tongue duelling with his. He relished the taste and feel of her, the energy of her body awakening the sleeping dragon of need he had suppressed for so long. Hot tongues of flame licked through him, scorching him inside and out, making him so hard he couldn't think about anything but getting her to the nearest flat surface so he could drive himself into her honeyed warmth.

'I shouldn't be doing this,' he groaned as he pulled his mouth off hers to nibble on the soft skin of her neck.

'Neither should I,' she whispered back huskily as she gently nipped at his bottom lip, her tongue flicking where her teeth had caught him. 'I'm not supposed to dating.'

'This wasn't a date,' he said returning to her mouth to press a series of kisses to its cushioned surface. 'We just went out to dinner with my kid sister as chaperone.'

Georgie kissed his lips once, twice, three times. 'Maybe we should stop now…'

'Yeah,' he said, and, smothering a groan, crushed her mouth beneath his again.

'Ahem.' The sound of someone clearing their throat came from the front door of the apartment block.

Georgie sprang out of Ben's arms, her cheeks going pink when she saw Rhiannon looking at her with her arms folded reprovingly.

'It's not what you think,' Georgie began.

Rhiannon ignored her to introduce herself to the tall, silent figure standing to one side. 'Hi, I'm Georgie's flatmate, Rhiannon Taylor.'

'Pleased to meet you, Rhiannon,' he said politely, offering her a hand. 'Ben Blackwood.'

'I've heard a lot about you,' Rhiannon said with a cryptic smile.

'I hope it wasn't all bad,' Ben said with a little glance in Georgie's direction.

'On the contrary, it was all good,' Rhiannon said. 'Jules Littlemore, your intern, is a friend of mine, and Georgie's, too, actually. Jules has told me how much he enjoys working with you.'

'It was kind of him to say so,' Ben answered. 'He's a hard worker.' He pushed a hand through his hair and added, 'I'd better be going. Hannah's probably run out of friends to text by now. Nice to meet you, Rhiannon.'

He turned to Georgie. 'I'll see you in Theatre tomorrow at eight-thirty. Goodnight.'

'Goodnight…'

Rhiannon waited until Ben's car had driven away before turning to face Georgie with a victorious look on her face. 'I *knew* it! I just knew you couldn't do it. You're hopeless when it comes to handsome men.'

'I told you before, it wasn't really a date,' Georgie growled as she stomped towards the lift.

'Yeah, and I bet you're going to say that wasn't really a kiss either,' Rhiannon said with a teasing grin. 'Come on, pay up, Georgie. You owe me one thousand dollars.'

The lift doors opened and they stepped in together.

'I don't mind paying you the money but I'm not officially involved with Ben Blackwood,' Georgie insisted. 'Besides, he's not over his last girlfriend.'

'He didn't look like he was missing her too much back there when he was kissing you,' Rhiannon pointed out wryly.

Georgie rolled her eyes. 'You know what men are like,' she said. 'Look at what Andrew was getting up to with me while he was supposedly getting over *his* ex.'

'Good point,' Rhiannon said, chewing at her lip for a moment. 'What say we wait and see what happens before you pay me?'

Georgie whooshed out a despondent breath as the lift doors opened on their floor. 'Nothing's going to happen,' she said.

Rhiannon just smiled.

CHAPTER FIFTEEN

GEORGIE didn't leave anything to chance the next morning and left extra early so she could turn up on time in Theatre for Emma Stanley's case. She had found it hard to sleep the previous night, thinking about the young girl who had so much at stake, not to mention Ben, who as Emma's neurosurgeon had so much pressure on him to perform a miracle when the chance of one was not very likely.

Linda greeted her as she came into the change room. 'Tough morning this one,' she said. 'Ben's really feeling it. He hides it pretty well but I've worked with him long enough to know the signs.'

'He told me about the case yesterday,' Georgie said as she put her bag into one of the lockers. 'It's hard, what life tosses up, isn't it?'

'Sure is,' Linda agreed. 'The parents are such lovely people who would move heaven and earth to get their daughter back to full health. I only hope Ben can pull this one off. Mind you, if anyone can, he can. He's got that steely determination to succeed where others would have given up long ago. I have a feeling your father saw that quality in him right from the start.'

Georgie frowned. 'What do you mean?'

Linda hung up her blouse before turning to face her. 'Your father would never have failed someone unless he thought they weren't quite ready to face the responsibility of being the one to make life-and-death decisions, as neurosurgeons sometimes have to do. I reckon your father thought Ben needed that extra six months of study to further develop his patience and skill.'

'I wish Ben could see it that way,' Georgie said as she reached for a coat hanger.

Linda gave her a confident smile. 'He will eventually,' she said. 'Especially now.'

Georgie could feel Ben's tension as soon as she walked into Theatre. His eyes looked tired as if he hadn't slept well and he kept cracking his knuckles as he waited for David Lucas, the anaesthetist, to finish preparing Emma for surgery.

Georgie met Ben's gaze, holding it for a beat or two, hoping he could feel her support coming from deep within her.

The young girl was finally anaesthetised, catheterised and placed in the prone position on the operating table, supported by padded rests and sandbags. Needle electrodes were placed into the major muscles of each leg and attached to an EMG monitor.

'I will be using a nerve stimulator during the surgery to assist with identifying and preserving the spinal nerve roots as they are dissected free of the tumour,' Ben explained in a calm, even tone.

Georgie stood by his side and watched with bated breath as he prepped Emma's back with alcohol and chlorhexidine and draped the area, leaving the lumbar region exposed and placing a steridrape on the operative area. He made a midline incision over the L2 to L5 regions and carried it down with diathermy to the spinous processes of the lumbar spine, inserting two self-retraining retractors.

'On each side I'm cutting through the spinal pedicles,' he said, removing the spinous processes of L3 and L4 to reveal the bulge in the dura caused by the tumour.

Georgie could see the tangle of nerve roots and tumour and felt her heart sink again at how tough a call this was going to be for both Emma and Ben.

She thought again about her conversation with Linda in the change rooms. Ben certainly had an edge when it came to gritty determination. He had worked long and hard to get through medical school and his specialist training. Obstacles had been put in his way right from the word go but he had soldiered on regardless.

He was doing it now, she realised as she saw the way his hands worked with meticulous precision, his concentration fierce, but his manner professionally calm and controlled.

Three and a half hours later, using a combination of painstaking dissection, wearing magnifying loops and using the nerve stimulator, Ben peeled away the tumour from each nerve root, eventually freeing the whole mass. The motor function to the lower limbs seemed intact, according to the positive spikes on the EMG monitor, but Georgie knew that there was no way of effectively monitoring nerves to the bowels, bladder or sensation. Only in the post-operative period would it become clear if Emma had suffered any neurological deficit. Not only that, it could take a year or more to be certain whether any deficit was temporary or permanent.

Ben put on two titanium plates and screws, one on each side of the remaining pedicles, to replace the strength lost when the laminae and spinous processes were removed, and he then assisted Georgie in placing a small closed suction drain into the wound before closing it.

The relief when it was all over was palpable.

Georgie met his eyes over his mask and shield, the flicker of doubt and hope fighting it out in those dark blue depths, making her heart suddenly contract.

'You did a good job assisting,' he said as Emma was wheeled out to Recovery.

'Thanks,' she said softly. 'You were amazingly patient. I couldn't believe how difficult it would be to preserve every nerve root.'

He stripped off his mask and gave her a tired smile. 'I had a good teacher,' he said.

'My father, you mean?'

'You sound surprised.'

'I am, considering what you've said about him being difficult to work with,' she admitted.

'He was a nightmare to work with at times but that doesn't mean he wasn't a fine neurosurgeon,' he said, tossing his gloves in the bin. 'He may have thrown a few instruments in his time but as far as patience with a patient went, he was hard to beat. I've seen him stand in one spot for ten hours to remove a spinal tumour.'

'Emma's parents are waiting to speak to you,' Linda informed him from the door.

'Right,' he said, and left Georgie standing there with her mouth open.

She met Jules coming out of the lift as she was heading up to the high-dependency unit to check on Emma, who had been transferred there from Recovery.

'I hear you've lost the bet,' he said with a grin, 'and with the boss, no less. Way to go, girl.'

She gave him a withering look. 'I am *not* dating Ben,' she said with cutting emphasis.

'Better announce it on the hospital loudspeaker, then,' he advised. 'It was the hot topic in the doctors' room this morning. Everyone seems to think you are.'

'Oh, no!' she groaned.

'Madeleine Brothers wasn't too happy about it,' he went on. 'She thinks it's going to cause more trouble with Mr Tander.'

'How is Mrs Tander?' Georgie asked. 'Mr Blackwood advised me to stay out of ICU until things settle down a bit.'

'She's not doing too well,' Jules said. 'Mr Blackwood ordered a whole-body CT scan but she's too unstable to take down to X-Ray. The police have been in to talk to Mr Tander once or twice. He's pretty annoyed about it so you'd better do as the boss says and keep your head down.'

'Does Ben…er…I mean Mr Blackwood think there's something else wrong with Mrs Tander?' Georgie asked. 'Something we might have missed in the initial assessment?'

'I guess he must if he wants a full scan done,' he said. Glancing at his watch, he added, 'I've got to dash. See you round some time.'

'Yeah.' Georgie answered absently. 'See you…'

'Dr Willoughby!' an irate male voice thundered from down the corridor. 'Just the person I want to see. How dare you insinuate that I tried to kill my wife?'

Georgie felt her stomach go hollow. Jonathon Tander was livid, his whole body pulsating as he cornered her.

'The police have been on my back all morning, thanks to you,' he railed. 'I'm going to sue you. Do you hear me? I am going to have you dismissed from this hospital for the precious rumours you've circulated about me. You will never work again in any hospital.'

'Mr Tander, I—'

'I love my wife,' he cut her off, tears suddenly brimming in his bloodshot eyes. 'She's everything to me. I love her. I would never allow her to suffer…'

Georgie felt as if her heart was being squeezed as the man's broken sobs sounded from deep within his chest. His whole body shook with the force of them, his legs trembling so much she was sure he was going to fall in a heap on the floor.

'Mr Tander,' she said, putting a gentle hand on his arm in order to lead him to a chair, 'please, sit down and let me try to explain.'

He wrenched his arm away from her and glared at her through his tears. 'Don't try and butter me up. You're making things so much worse, don't you realise that? So much worse. She's suffered enough. I can't take any more. Oh, God, I can't take any more…'

'It's all right, Georgie.' Ben's deep voice spoke from behind her. 'Wait for me in my office. I'll deal with this.'

Georgie backed away, her emotions see-sawing as she heard him deal gently with the older man.

'Come on, Mr Tander,' he said. 'Let's get you a hot cup of tea and some time to yourself in one of the lounges.'

'I love her,' Mr Tander said as he walked with Ben back towards the lifts, his voice a wobbly whisper. 'I would do anything for her…anything…'

'I know you would,' Ben answered softly as he pushed the lift call button. 'That's what life is all about—loving people. And it hurts at times.'

Georgie was on her way to Ben's office when she was intercepted by Richard DeBurgh.

'Ah, Georgie, my dear,' he said, 'I've been meaning to have a little chat with you about something. Have you got a minute?'

'Sure,' she said, 'but I haven't got much time. I have to meet Mr Blackwood in a few minutes.'

Richard opened his office door and waved her through. 'Come in and make yourself comfortable. Ben won't mind waiting.'

Georgie took the chair opposite his desk but, instead of sitting in his own chair, he perched on the edge of his desk. She tried to edge away but the chair's legs wouldn't slide on the thick carpet.

'Word is circulating that you and Ben are an item,' he said, running his gaze over her. 'Is it true?'

She moistened her suddenly dry lips. 'Not really...'

He arched one brow. 'Define what you mean by "not really",' he said.

'I'd rather not discuss my personal life as it's—'

He gave a chuckle that somehow wasn't reflected in his eyes. 'None of my business, right?'

Georgie couldn't even crack a smile in return. 'That's right,' she said a little stiffly.

He leaned closer. 'Listen to me, Georgie. You're making a big mistake, getting involved with Ben. What will your father say?'

She put her chin up but her confidence was already starting to sag. 'He'll be happy if I am happy.'

Richard shook his head at her. 'Somehow I can't see your father accepting Ben Blackwood as a future son-in-law,' he said. 'Have you told him about your relationship with the man he thought would never make it as a neurosurgeon?'

She gritted her teeth and said, 'I am *not* having a relationship with Mr Blackwood and I think my father *did* think he would make it. He just wanted Ben to have a few more months to hone his skills.'

'You seem like a sensible girl, Georgie,' he said. 'Don't

waste yourself on someone like Ben Blackwood. If you're after a quick little affair to boost your career prospects, come and see me. I'd be more than happy to oblige.'

Georgie stared at him in shock, wondering if she had heard correctly. 'Excuse me?' she said, narrowing her eyes slightly.

His smile was smooth but again didn't involve his eyes. 'I met your ex-partner, Andrew McNally, at an old boys' function from the cathedral school we both attended. He told me all about you.' He paused as his gaze slid over her before adding, 'About how much fun you were.'

She felt her throat go dry as she scrambled to her feet. 'I think you've got the wrong idea, Mr DeBurgh,' she said, and headed for the door.

'Think about it, Georgie,' he called out after her. 'I'll leave the offer open if you change your mind.'

She answered by closing the door firmly behind her.

'What's wrong?' Rhiannon asked as soon as Georgie came into the apartment that evening. 'You look like you're about to throttle someone.'

Georgie began to pace the room. 'I am *so* angry I could scream,' she ground out furiously. 'That obnoxious *creep!* How could I have got it so wrong about him? He's nothing but a sleazy silver-tongued snake.'

'So what did Ben do now?' Rhiannon asked.

Georgie stopped pacing, her face draining of colour when she suddenly remembered she was supposed to have been waiting in Ben's office for him. 'Oh, no!'

'What's wrong?'

'I was supposed to meet Ben in his office and I completely forgot when one of the senior surgeons came on to me.' She gave a little shudder and added, 'Ben warned me about him but I thought he had it completely wrong.'

'*Eeuw, gross!*' Rhiannon said with feeling. 'Why don't you report him for sexual harassment?'

'I might just do that,' Georgie said as she reached for her mobile and dialled Ben's number, but it went straight to the message service. She put the phone back in her bag and let out a frustrated sigh. 'I wish I could see him face to face to explain.'

'Do you know which apartment block he lives in?' Rhiannon asked.

'No, but I'll ask the hospital switchboard,' Georgie answered, and reached for her phone again.

CHAPTER SIXTEEN

BEN answered the door with a towel hitched around his hips his hair still dripping from his shower.

'Oh…sorry…' Georgie bit her lip and tried to keep her eyes north of the border. 'Um…I picked a bad time to drop in on you…'

'Not at all,' he said, stepping aside to let her in. 'I just got back from the gym.' He closed the door and added, 'I thought I might have seen you there. You didn't hang around at the hospital so I thought you'd gone straight there.'

'I'm so sorry I didn't keep our appointment,' she said. 'I got a bit distracted by…by something that happened just after I left you with Mr Tander.'

He frowned as he looked down at her. 'Jonathan Tander didn't have another go at you, did he? I left him with the hospital chaplain in the relatives' lounge. Did he somehow track you down again?'

She shook her head and cupped her elbows with her crossed-over hands. 'I had a bit of a run-in with Richard DeBurgh…well, not exactly a run-in, more of a misunderstanding…of sorts…'

'What sort of misunderstanding?'

Georgie stared at the droplets of water trickling down his

uscular chest, her stomach tilting with the desire to follow
ach one with the tip of her tongue. How would he taste? She
ondered. Salty or tangy or…

'Georgie?' he prompted.

She dragged her eyes up to his. 'He offered me an affair,'
he told him bluntly.

His frown deepened. 'He *what?*'

'He seemed to think I would be interested in giving my
areer a bit of a boost by sleeping with him,' she said.

'You should report him.'

'I'm still thinking about it.'

'You have enough to deal with right now without unwanted
ttention from men who should know better,' he said, raking
hand through his damp hair, leaving deep finger grooves in
e jet-black strands.

'It's all right, Ben. I can handle men like Richard. Heaven
nows, I've met plenty of them before.'

His eyes caught and held hers. 'I suppose you know the
umours are flying thick and fast about us at the hospital?'

She drew in a fluttering breath. 'Yes…I had heard some-
ing along those lines.'

'What do you think we should do about it?'

'I don't know…' She captured her bottom lip once more.
What do you think we should do?'

'We could deny it strenuously,' he said, looking down at
er mouth.

'I guess that could work…'

'Of course, it didn't help that we were seen by your
latmate, who has no doubt told my intern.'

'No,' she said, rolling her lips together for a moment.
You're right. That wouldn't have helped at all.'

'Or we could go along with it,' he suggested. 'You know,
retend we really *are* having an affair.'

She looked at him, unable to think of anything to say.

'When you think about it, it could solve your problem with Richard DeBurgh,' he said. 'He'll back off once he hear we're officially seeing each other.'

'So…' She ran her tongue over her dry lips before continuing. 'What you're suggesting is we *pretend* to be dating, right'.

'Yeah, why not?' he said. 'You can let your flatmate in on th secret so you don't lose the bet, but to all intents and purpose everyone else will believe we're having a bit of a fling.'

She frowned at him. 'And you don't have a problem with that?'

'Why should I have a problem with it? We're both adults The fact that you're my registrar is neither here nor there Work is work and play is play.'

'But we're not really playing,' she pointed out. 'We're just pretending.'

'Is that disappointment I hear in your tone?'

'Of course not!' she insisted. 'Why on earth would I b disappointed?'

He stepped closer, his warm, damp body almost touchin hers. 'We could be pretty hot together, don't you think Georgie?' he said in a low sexy rumble. 'When we kissed las night I was so close to—'

She blocked his next word with her fingertip. 'No,' she sai quickly and huskily. 'Don't say it…it's like tempting fate.'

He captured her finger and sucked on it—hard—his eye holding hers in the magnetic force field of his. 'We ca pretend or we can do it for real. Right now I'm thinking rea would be good.'

'No…' she said, her stomach somersaulting as his tongu rolled over her fingertip. 'No, it wouldn't be good. We're nc right for each other. You know we're not. You said i yourself—we come from completely different backgrounds

He blew his hot breath into the shell of her ear, his tongue snaking out to trace its delicate contours until her spine threatened to dissolve. 'Haven't you heard of the expression opposites attract"?'

'Yes...' She shivered as his mouth hovered just above hers. 'But it doesn't mean it will last.'

'I don't know about that,' he said, trailing a pathway of kisses down the side of her neck. 'We could make it last.'

'F-for how long?' she asked, as her whole body shivered in reaction.

His hands skated over the swell of her breasts, his eyes burning into hers. 'How long do you want it to last?' he asked.

'I...I don't want to waste time on going-nowhere relationships,' she said, running her hands over his chest, her fingertips relishing the hard contours of his body. 'I'm twenty-seven years old. I have four years of study ahead of me. It's...complicated...'

He planted a hot-as-fire kiss on her mouth. 'We could take one step at a time,' he said.

'I'm not ready for big steps...'

'Baby steps, then,' he said, capturing her bottom lip between his teeth and tugging gently. 'Little tiny baby steps.'

Georgie could feel herself melting inside and out. Her legs were like two soggy noodles and her spine loosened to the point of collapse. 'This is very tempting...' she breathed.

She felt his smile like an imprint on her lips. 'It's supposed to be tempting,' he said. 'I want to sleep with you. I think I've wanted it from the moment you put that hard collar on me when you knocked me down. You've been keeping me awake more than my most difficult patients, do you realise that?'

She raised her mouth just enough to secure contact with his, lifting them off only long enough to say, 'I think I've wanted you from the moment you called me Georgiana.'

He looked at her quizzically. 'I thought you didn't like being called by your full name?'

'I don't, but the way you said it made me want to grab you and shake you. I was so angry.'

'But you're not angry at me now?'

She looked at the sensual curve of his mouth. 'No, I'm not angry.'

'So what are you feeling?' he asked after a two-beat pause.

'I'm feeling like I'm sinking in over my head,' she confessed as his breath caressed her face. 'I want to step forward but I'm scared I'm going to make another big mistake.'

'Don't be scared, sweetheart,' he said, cupping her face with his hand. 'Let's just take things slowly.'

'Slowly sounds good,' Georgie said as he kissed her neck again, each whisper-soft press of his lips making her shiver all over again.

'Is this slow enough for you?' he asked, as he began a leisurely exploration of her bottom lip with the tip of his tongue.

Her belly exploded with desire at the exquisite touch, her legs sagging beneath her. 'Maybe we could speed it up a tiny bit,' she said as her tongue brushed against his.

'How much?' he asked, pulling on her top lip this time with his mouth, in a tug and release action that sent a hot river of sensation rushing down her spine.

She pressed herself closer, the heated trajectory of his erection sending her into a tailspin. She opened her mouth as his came down, whimpering softly as his tongue swept hers up into a toe-curling duel that left her totally breathless.

His hands cupped her bottom and pulled her into his hardness, the pulsing urgency of his body making her wonder how she had resisted him this long. Was it possible to fall in love so rapidly? she wondered. She had made the mistake before of allowing physical attraction to take precedence, but

omehow with Ben she knew her feelings for him were not
ust physical. He was everything she most admired in a man.
He might come from a completely different background from
ers but he had qualities that made every other man she'd
ated seem shallow and self-serving in comparison.

'Am I going too fast?' Ben asked as he cupped her breast
with the warmth of his palm.

'No,' she said, looking dreamily into his smouldering gaze.
'Not fast enough.'

He rubbed his thumb over the tight point of her nipple,
ack and forth in a caressing movement that made her ache
o feel his hand on her without the barrier of clothes. 'If I
peed up, I might not be able to stop,' he warned. 'You have
his amazing effect on me, Dr Willoughby. I can't seem to
ontrol myself around you.'

She smiled as she nestled closer to him. 'You have the
ame effect on me. I feel like ripping that towel off your body
nd kissing you all over.'

'Don't let me stop you,' he said, holding his hands up in
urrender. 'Go ahead, make my day.'

She trailed her fingers down his chest, lingering over each
ark brown pebbly nipple, pressing her mouth to each one,
olling her tongue over them in turn, her stomach kicking in
xcitement when she heard his groan of pleasure rumble from
leep within his chest.

'Am I going too fast for you, Mr Blackwood?' she asked
playfully, tiptoeing her fingertips to the trail of dark hair that
went from his navel to beneath the precariously hung towel.

'Not fast enough,' he growled, and, picking her up in his
rms, he carried her to his bedroom, knocking over a lamp
n his haste.

Georgie helped him remove her clothes with fumbling
ingers that shook in anticipation. She gasped when his hands

found her naked skin, the feel of his palms on her breasts a
he explored them making her breath catch in her throat. Hi
touch was gentle but determined, tender and yet urgent.

'God, I can't believe I'm doing this,' he groaned as h
brought his mouth to her breast, his hot breath dancing over th
aching point of her nipple. 'You should be pushing me away.

She arched her body as his mouth closed over her nipple
'Do you want me to push you away?'

'No,' he groaned, as he moved to her other breast. 'You'v
got the most beautiful body. I've been lying awake at nigh
thinking of how you looked in that barely there bikini o
yours. Just as well my sister was there otherwise I would hav
been doing this then.'

She gasped as his hands moved to the final lacy barrier tha
shielded her femininity from his burning gaze. He hooked on
finger in the elastic of her knickers and pulled them down, hi
hand cupping her gently as she pulsed with longing against him

She gasped again when he slowly inserted one of his lon;
fingers into her silky warmth, the tantalising movement mim
icking what he longed to do with his aroused length. She
reached down between them to pull away the towel that wa
still covering him, her stomach tilting in delight when she fel
his naked body pressing against her skin. Her hands skate
over him, touching him, exploring his hard contours, her fin
gertip encountering the bead of moisture that signalled hov
very aroused he was.

He pulled her hand away and covered her mouth with his
the weight of his body on hers making her feel utterly
feminine and totally desirable as his hard thighs wrappe
around hers. She could feel his body probing for entry but h
kept control, his kiss deepening until she was writhing beneat
him.

He tore his mouth off hers long enough to reach across he

o the bedside drawer in search of a condom. He rustled around the drawer for ages before he finally found one, holding it up with a victorious grin. 'For a moment there I thought we were going to have to suspend proceedings while I dashed out to the pharmacy down the road for supplies.'

Georgie was somehow touched that she was the first woman he had considered making love with since his break-up. It was a nice feeling to know he hadn't been bedding every woman he could in the past nine months. It made her feel incredibly special.

She ran her hands over his flat stomach as she watched him put on the condom, her belly flip-flopping all over again at the sight of him fully aroused.

He kissed her again, his mouth full of sensual promise as it moved down her body, until he came to her tender folds hidden behind a tiny landing strip of dark curls. She drew in a sharp little breath when his tongue parted her, the sensation of his mouth on her most secret place sending her heart rate way out of her training zone. She clutched at his silky dark head as he subjected her to a passionate assault on her senses, every nerve jangling and screaming for release. The tension built and built until with a cut-off cry she came, her body arching and jerking beneath his exquisite caress.

'Good?' he asked as he moved over her to settle between her still trembling thighs.

'The best…' she breathed in wonder as her eyes locked with his. 'I've never been able to…you know…do it that way…'

His dark eyes glinted with satisfaction. 'Like I said before, Georgie, you press my buttons so it's only fair I press yours.'

She let out a rapturous gasp as he entered her in a single thrust, her body grabbing at him greedily, wanting all of him to fill her aching need. 'Oh…wow…'

'Too fast?' he asked, his breathing becoming rapid.

'No… It's just you feel so…so…so good.'

'It's feeling pretty good from my side, too,' he said, trying to hold back. 'I'm going to come too soon if you don't stop wriggling like that against me.'

'I want you to come,' she said, grabbing at his buttocks and digging her fingers in.

'We're supposed to be taking things slowly,' he said, speeding up.

'I know…' she panted, as she began to climb the summit again.

'Whose idea was that anyway?' he said, as he felt himself teetering on the edge.

'I can't remember,' she gasped as he surged deeply, filling her completely. 'I think it might have been mine. Dumb, huh?'

'You're not dumb, baby, you're gorgeous.' He sucked in a harsh breath. 'And I think I'm losing control here.'

She arched up to meet his next downward thrust, her whole world splintering into a thousand pieces, her cry of release just a couple of seconds ahead of his. She felt the shudders of his release reverberate through his body where it was pressed against hers, the pumping action of his pelvis so deliciously male she shivered all over with delight.

She held him close, her fingers caressing his hair, his neck and his shoulders, her heart rate struggling to return to normal.

So this was what being in love felt like, she thought in amazement. No wonder she'd got it so wrong with Andrew. She mentally cringed as she thought about the few times they had made love, almost mechanically, as if following a manual. There had been no emotional connection, no meeting on a level that was beyond the physical.

Ben eased himself up on his elbows to look down at her. He tucked a wayward strand of her hair behind her ear with touch so gentle Georgie felt tears prickling at the backs of her eyes. 'A guy could get pretty used to having you look at him like that,' he said.

She smiled as she traced her fingertip over the curve of his top lip. 'A girl could get pretty used to having a guy look at her the way you do at me,' she responded softly.

He pressed a soft-as-a-feather kiss to each of her eyelids before asking, 'So that crazy idea of mine of pretending we're having an affair is off, then, huh?'

'What's a thousand dollars anyway?' she said with a smile. 'It was worth it.'

He grinned as he brought his mouth back down to within a breath of hers. 'How many condoms do you think you could buy with a thousand dollars?'

'I don't know. How many do you think?'

'Let's start counting,' he said and took her to paradise once more.

CHAPTER SEVENTEEN

'ONE hundred, two hundred, three hundred—'

'Stop,' Rhiannon said as Georgie counted out the hundred-dollar bills the following morning. 'I have something to confess.'

Georgie let the next note flutter to the table. 'What?'

Rhiannon bit her lip. 'I've been seeing someone.'

Georgie's eyes went out on stalks. *You have?*

Rhiannon nodded. 'I was going to tell you a couple of days ago but I wasn't sure if the guy felt the same way about me. We weren't really dating…sort of catching up…' She gave a little grimace and added, 'Sorry.'

'Who is it?' Georgie asked. 'Anyone I know?'

'Jules Littlemore.'

Georgie gaped at her. *Jules?*

'Why are you so surprised? He's a really decent man. I know he's a couple of years younger than me but I've always liked him and when he kissed me I sort of…fell in love with him.'

'I'm really glad for you, Rhiannon,' Georgie said. 'Jules is a great guy and perfect for you when I think about it.'

'So you're not angry at me?'

'No,' she said, smiling at her flatmate. 'It was a stupid bet in the first place.'

'So this relationship you're having with Ben Blackwood is serious?' Rhiannon asked.

Georgie had to wait until her belly stopped quivering in reaction to the very mention of his name. 'We're taking it one day at a time,' she said. 'We're going to keep it quiet at the hospital for as long as we can. It will be difficult but we want to enjoy getting to know one another before we announce it to all and sundry.'

'You've got that look on your face.'

'What look?'

'That dreamy I'm-in-love sort of look.'

'I *am* in love,' Georgie answered. 'But this time I know it's for real.'

Rhiannon frowned. 'But he's not blond.'

Georgie rolled her eyes. 'That's a truckload of nonsense, and you know it.'

'It's not!' Rhiannon insisted. 'Madame Celestia told me I would fall in love with someone I had known for years. She said I wouldn't recognise him until Jupiter was in Venus…or was it Mars? I can't quite remember. All I know is she has—'

'Totally ripped you off,' Georgie said, taking the money off the table.

'Mock me all you like but I think she's onto something,' Rhiannon said with a little pout.

Georgie glanced at her watch. 'I've got to fly,' she said. 'I'm meeting Ben in his office before I go to Theatre with Mr Vinay, one of the other neurosurgeons.'

The traffic was like a clogged artery all the way to the hospital. Georgie sat drumming her fingers on the steering-wheel impatiently as she waited for the traffic lights to go through yet another change without a single car moving forward.

She hated the thought of wasting a minute when she could

be in Ben's arms again. He had made her feel so wonderful last night, so feminine and desirable. He had held her so tenderly, his breath feathering through her hair as he'd talked to her of his plans for the future. She had snuggled up close, breathing in the scent of their love-making, wondering if he felt even a fraction of what she felt for him. She certainly hoped so. He was so perfect for her in spite of what Rhiannon's clairvoyant said, she thought with a wry smile.

His office door was closed when she finally got there and her hand stopped mid-air as she went to knock when she heard voices inside.

Male and female voices.

'I love you, Ben,' the female voice was saying. 'I've always loved you. I made a terrible mistake in betraying you with my stupid little affair with Cain Osborne. You were so busy all the time and I felt neglected. I only got involved with him because he was so insistent and available and you were so distant. I know it was wrong but I felt so lonely waiting for you night after night.'

'Leila, please—'

'No,' Leila said. 'You have to listen to me, darling. Cain left me. It's over, well and truly. I don't love him like I love you. I never did. I want us to try again.'

Georgie felt her heart come to a clunking stop in her chest. She broke out in a cold sweat as the silence in the room lengthened.

Why was Ben taking so long to answer?

'We were great together, Ben,' Leila went on. 'Surely you can't deny it? Let's start again but this time let's do it properly.'

Another too-long silence.

'So what you're saying is you want to get married?' Ben finally asked.

Georgie felt her knees give way and had to hold onto the wall to keep herself upright, the sound of her blood roaring in her ears.

'Yes, Ben,' Leila said softly. 'That's exactly what I'm saying. Let's get married and have the family you've always wanted.'

Georgie had heard enough. Why hadn't Ben told Leila he was involved with someone else? She stumbled away with her heart in tatters, her stomach rolling with nausea at how stupid she had been to fall in love with yet another man who had unfinished business with an ex-partner.

'What's taking Mr Blackwood so long this morning?' the nurse on duty, Loretta Harold, asked Georgie as she joined the rest of the neurosurgical team for the first post-operative day ward round.

'I'm sure he'll be here as soon as he can,' Georgie said, as she looked towards the bed where Emma was lying, dozing, her small figure looking pale and heart-wrenchingly vulnerable.

'Here he is now,' one of the medical students said as Ben walked in through the door.

Georgie concentrated on Emma's chart before handing it back to Loretta, who was already filling in Ben on the details.

'Emma had a restless night, finally getting to sleep in the early hours of the morning after enough morphine to knock out a footballer. She's one tough kid.'

'Emma, are you awake?' Ben asked as he touched the young girl on the arm.

Emma stirred and groaned and then half opened her eyes to take in the three doctors, three students and a nurse standing around the end of her bed. 'Am I OK?' she asked.

'Emma, the operation went very well,' Ben said. 'I've spoken to your parents. They've been sitting by your bed most of the night, and have only just gone home to get some sleep themselves. They'll be back in this afternoon.'

Emma tried to sit up, but winced in pain and slumped back down on the pillows. 'Did you get all of the tumour out, Dr Blackwood?' she asked in a scratchy voice.

'I think so, Emma. We took a long time, nearly four hours, looking for every spot of the tumour and trying not to damage any of the spinal nerves. But we have to see if there is any damage by testing the power and sensation in your lower limbs and trunk,' he explained.

'Will I be able to run and compete again?'

In spite of her anger towards him, Georgie felt for Ben at that moment. There was no way of knowing at this point whether Emma would even walk, let alone run. She could see the tension on his face, even though he did his best to conceal it. No specialist liked being the harbinger of bad news and certainly not to a young active person.

'I hope so, Emma,' he said. 'Now, can we see if you can wiggle your toes on both feet?'

Emma concentrated, looking hard at the feet as she tried to move them, but the toes remained immobile. 'Nothing's happening, Mr Blackwood,' she said, clearly starting to panic as her eyes widened with fear. 'I'm trying to move my toes but it's as if the message isn't getting through.'

'OK, let's try tensing your thigh muscles,' Ben said calmly

Emma concentrated again, and this time there was a tiny flicker of movement in the quadriceps.

'That's good, Emma,' Ben said with visible relief. 'Your upper leg muscles are moving. The more peripheral nerves are hopefully intact but they may take a bit longer to recover I want you to try several times today to move each muscle in both legs, and I'll see you again tomorrow. It might take several weeks for full recovery and then some physiotherapy to regain your muscle strength. When we've finished our ward round today, my registrar Georgie Willoughby is going

o come back and document muscle movements more fully
and map out the sensation in the legs. But from what I can
see at the moment, we have at least a good chance that the
nerves are functioning.'

He smiled at the young patient and added, 'You might
make the national athletics team yet, Emma.'

'I'll make it, Dr Blackwood,' Emma said with a fiery glint
of determination in her eyes. 'Even if I have to compete in a
wheelchair, I'm going to make it.'

He gave her shoulder a gentle squeeze. 'That's the spirit.
I'll see you tomorrow.'

Georgie followed him out of the room and tagged along
for the rest of the ward round, maintaining a low profile as
he discussed each patient's care with the medical students and
the intern. He barely addressed a single question her way,
which suited her perfectly. She caught his glance once or
twice but quickly looked away again and concentrated on the
patient being reviewed instead.

When the ward round came to an end she slipped away
to prepare for theatre with Sankil Vinay, one of the other
neurosurgeons.

Linda met up with Georgia in the change rooms after the
routine list. 'I was hoping to have a quiet word with you,' she
said. 'Are you OK? You seemed a little upset when you came
into Mr Vinay's theatre earlier.'

'I'm fine,' Georgie answered with forced brightness in her
tone. 'We had a tough day in Theatre yesterday. The young
track-and-field girl, Emma Stanley, really got to me, but
I'm feeling a little better now that she's got some muscle
movement.'

'Yes, I heard about her,' Linda said. 'Ben is amazing,
isn't he?'

Georgie averted her gaze to concentrate on folding her theatre scrubs into a neat little pile. 'Yes…he is.'

'Is it true you're seeing him?' Linda asked after a moment's hesitation.

Georgie turned and looked at the theatre nurse eye to eye. 'No, it's not true,' she said. 'I'm actually seeing someone else.'

Linda looked surprised. 'Who?'

'Jules Littlemore,' she answered, mentally asking Rhiannon to forgive her, not to mention Jules, whose eye she had been trying to catch on the ward round that morning. He had looked at her quizzically once or twice but she hadn't been able to take him to one side to discuss her situation with him. She only hoped she could track him down before the hospital grapevine did.

'Oh…' Linda looked a little bewildered. 'I must have got my wires crossed or something. I was sure I heard you and Ben were having a relationship.'

'It happens all the time in hospitals,' Georgie said. 'Stories get twisted.' She felt guilty for lying, but she wasn't really thinking straight. Her emotions were in tatters.

'Yes…' Linda said, frowning as she took off her paper overshoes. 'That must have been what happened.'

'Jules, quick,' Georgie said, grabbing at the intern's shirt front outside A and E a short time later. 'You have to help me.'

'What's wrong, Georgie?' Jules asked. He could see she'd been crying. 'You've been acting weird all morning with all that eye-flickering stuff. What's going on?'

She led him to a storage room off the corridor and quickly explained her dilemma. 'So, you see, I need you to pretend we're having a hot affair, just for a day or so, *please?*'

Jules looked doubtful. 'I don't know…'

'I'll pay you the thousand dollars Rhiannon's not getting, nd I'll clear it with her first.'

His cheeks went a dull shade of red. 'I guess she told you, uh?'

'Yes. So will you help me out?'

'A thousand bucks will come in really handy,' he said. 'I ust bought Rhiannon an engagement ring and my credit card s maxed out.' He took the ring out of his pocket and showed t to her. 'Do you think she'll like it?'

Georgie's happiness for her friends was spoilt by her own nisery, but she didn't let it show. 'It's beautiful,' she said. Have you asked her yet?'

'I was going to do it tonight,' he said. Looking worried, he dded, 'Do you think she'll say yes?'

She smiled and gave him a quick peck on the cheek. 'Of ourse she will,' she said. 'She's probably written it into the tars.'

Have you seen Georgie?' Ben asked Linda outside his oper-ting theatre close to lunchtime.

'Yes, she was doing a list of minor cases with Sankil Vinay earlier,' she answered. 'I was just talking to her in the hange rooms.'

'I have to see her about Emma Stanley's follow-up. Do you now where she is now?'

'Probably canoodling in some corridor somewhere with ules Littlemore,' she said.

Ben's brows snapped together. 'What?'

Linda folded her arms. 'She's having a fling with your ntern,' she said. 'She told me about fifteen minutes ago. And ere everyone was thinking she was dating you. It just goes o show the danger of listening to idle gossip, doesn't it?'

Ben felt his gut begin to tighten but he forced himself to

relax. Surely Georgie had only said that to put Linda off. They'd agreed to keep their relationship quiet for a few weeks—that had to be the explanation.

It *had* to be.

It wasn't, he realised less than ten minutes later when he walked into the doctors' room and found his intern and his registrar in an embrace next to the coffee-machine. Anger rose in him so swiftly he had trouble containing his reaction. He closed the door with a sharp click and asked in a cool tone, 'Is there any coffee left for anyone else, or have you two taken the lot?'

Ben watched as Georgie stepped out of Jules's arms, her chin at that imperious angle he found so irritating, her expression showing not even a hint of remorse.

'Oops,' she said with a coy smile. 'It looks like our secret is out, Jules.'

'Er…yes…' Jules said, flushing slightly.

Ben ground his teeth behind his cold smile. 'If you want to keep your relationship a secret, you should pretend to be involved with someone else. Believe me, it works like a charm.'

'That's a good idea,' Jules said, wincing as the door snapped shut on Ben's exit.

Georgie blew out a breath and flopped into the nearest chair. 'I think I'm going to cry, but if I start I'm not sure I'm going to be able to stop.'

Jules patted her on the shoulder. 'You'll find someone else, Georgie.'

'I don't want anyone else.' She choked back a sob. 'Why do all the men I fall in love with have to already belong to someone else?'

'I hear Jules Littlemore is going out with Georgie Willoughby,' Madeleine said to Ben the following day.

Ben got to his feet and paced his office, which was diffi

cult to do in the limited space. It only took two strides and he had to turn back. 'I want her off my unit,' he bit out. 'I can't work with her.'

Madeleine's thin brows lifted. 'She's really got under your skin, hasn't she?'

He turned to face her, his expression dark with brooding anger. 'She had the audacity to sleep with me the night before she came out about her relationship with him. Can you believe that?'

'That's young women of today for you,' Madeleine said. 'They're sexually aggressive and have the morals of alley cats.'

He shoved a hand through his hair. 'I bet her father thinks she's an angel. God, I wish I could tell him what a little tart he has for a daughter.'

'She's not worth it, Ben,' she said. 'Look at the trouble she's already caused. Mr Tander is close to a nervous breakdown over her accusations, poor man.'

Ben frowned as he sat down. 'I organised for Marianne Tander to have a whole body CAT scan,' he said. 'But she's not well enough to be moved to X-Ray.'

'Have you got access to her medical records?'

'I'm working on it as we speak,' he said. 'I've got my secretary doing a ring around of the three major pathology labs to see if any bloods have been done on her in the last few months. The results should be faxed through in the next day or so, if not sooner.'

'I saw Leila earlier today,' Madeleine said after a small silence. 'She looked pretty upset. She didn't even acknowledge me on the way past.'

'She came to see me about getting back together,' he said, frowning slightly. 'The guy she was seeing left her.'

Madeleine's brows lifted again. 'So are you going to resume your relationship with her?'

He sat back in his chair. 'If anyone had asked me that even two weeks ago I would have probably given it some thought,' he admitted.

'Do you still feel anything for her?'

He let out a long-winded sigh. 'I don't understand the women of today,' he said, knowing he wasn't really answering her question. 'They blow hot and cold until you don't know what they want or feel.'

'Not all women are like that,' Madeleine said with a meaningful look.

Ben tried to let her down gently with a polite but distant smile. 'I'm off dating,' he said. 'No dates for three months minimum…no, make that six months. I swear to God if I go on a date with a woman before June I will donate five thousand dollars to the hospital research foundation.'

Madeleine smiled wistfully as she got to her feet. 'That sounds like a very good idea,' she said.

'Yeah…' Ben said once she'd left. Dragging a hand through his hair yet again, he added, 'It is. I don't know why I didn't think of it earlier.'

CHAPTER EIGHTEEN

'AREN'T you going to the gym any more?' Rhiannon asked two days later. 'This is the third day in a row you've missed.'

Georgie scrubbed at her red eyes. 'I don't want to run into Ben-Break-Your-Heart Blackwood,' she said. 'I'm going to switch my membership to another gym.'

'Poor you,' Rhiannon said, as she stroked Georgie's head. 'He really did a good job on you, didn't he?'

Georgie blew her nose and tucked the sodden tissue into her bra, joining the others for a lumpy potato effect. 'I'm so dumb when it comes to dating,' she said. 'I'm not going on another date for six months, I swear it.'

'That's a long time, Georgie.'

'I don't care,' she said as she got to her feet. 'If I so much as look at a man with a view to dating him, I'm going to donate a thousand dollars to the hospital research foundation…no, make that *five* thousand dollars. That should make me think twice before I fall into the same trap again.'

'Wow, that's a lot of money,' Rhiannon said.

Georgie set her shoulders determinedly. 'I know, but it'll be worth it to prove to myself that I can do it. I'm also going to pay my father back for the apartment.'

'But why? I mean, it was a present, wasn't it?' Rhiannon asked.

'That's not the point,' Georgie said. 'It's time I stood on my own two feet. It won't hurt me to pay my own way for once.'

Irene Clark, the head nurse on the unit, pulled Georgie to one side when she came to the ward the next morning. 'Ben asked me to tell you to meet him in his office,' she said. 'I think it's about you being transferred to another unit.'

Georgie had been expecting it so it didn't really come as much of a shock. She had considered asking for it herself but didn't want him to think she had any qualms about working with him. 'I'll go down now,' she said.

Ben picked up the thick wad of faxed results he had received and subsequently copied and sent to the police working on the investigation into Marianne Tander's accident. He'd not long finished speaking to the investigating officer who had filled him in on the background.

As much as Ben didn't want to see Georgie face to face, he thought she should be the first to know her suspicions had been correct after all.

Her heard her knock and called for her to come in, getting to his feet as she entered the room.

'You wanted to see me?' she said, nervously shifting from one foot to the other.

He frowned and noticed for the first time how red and bloodshot her eyes were. 'Have you been crying?' he asked.

'No,' she answered as her eyes moved away from his.

'I thought you should know you were right about Marianne Tander's injury,' he said into the tight silence.

Her eyes came back to his. 'Oh?'

'I researched her medical history,' he informed her. 'She has metastastic disease. She's been having chemotherapy for ovarian cancer. I confronted the husband this morning. It appears she and Jonathon made a pact. She made him promise that if she lived past Christmas, he was to help her die.'

Georgie put her hand to her throat. *'What?'*

He gave her a grim look. 'The plan was for her to take a dose of Valium and he would place a pillow over her face, but at the last minute he couldn't go through with it. I suspect the only reason he agreed to do it in the first place was that he didn't think she would last past Christmas, but she did and her suffering intensified to the point where she took matters into her own hands.'

Georgie's brow furrowed even further. 'So what happened?'

'Marianne Tander couldn't walk without assistance but the morning of the accident she somehow dragged herself to the staircase in their house and threw herself down just as Mr Tander was coming out of the bathroom. He couldn't get to her in time to stop her.'

'Oh, my God…the head wound was from the fall, right?'

He nodded. 'Mr Tander carried her out to his car and was on his way to the nearest hospital when due to his distraught state and the slippery conditions he briefly lost concentration and ran into the tree. When the police and ambulance arrived he panicked, wondering if they would accuse him of pushing her down the stairs, so on the spur of the moment made up the story about the other car. And, of course, luck was on his side as the roads were wet that morning and the police had been inundated with callouts to other accidents. There were no skid marks to verify his version of events. Apparently single-vehicle accidents are not always investigated unless there are concerns over injuries or death.'

Georgie sank to the chair opposite his desk. 'So what will happen to him? Mr Tander, I mean. Will he be charged?'

He let out a sigh as he pushed the results to one side. 'I'm not sure what charges if any will be laid,' he said. 'Marianne is going downhill fast. I don't think she'll see the week out. The cancer is so widespread I'm surprised she hasn't already gone into organ failure.'

Georgie chewed at her bottom lip for a moment. 'He really loves her…'

'Yes, he really does.'

'I was thinking about what he said when he cornered me that day,' she said. 'He said she'd suffered enough. Do you remember?'

He nodded. 'That's why I thought I'd run a check through the labs.'

Another silence tightened the air.

Georgie ran her tongue across her lips. 'Ben, I think I should tell you I overheard you and Leila discussing your relationship the other morning. I know I shouldn't have been eavesdropping at such a private moment but—'

'What?'

She winced at his sharp tone. 'I was just about to knock when I heard you both talking about putting the past aside and getting married.'

Ben stared at her. 'You *heard* that?'

She winced again. 'All of it. Sorry…'

Ben was starting to put two and two together, hope rising in his chest. 'So that little clinch in the doctors' room with Jules Littlemore? What was that all about?'

She bit her lip again. 'I'm not dating Jules. I was so upset I felt so used and wanted you think I was involved with Jules to hurt you. It was just like a replay of my relationship with Andrew, my ex. He was still in love with his previous girlfriend and when push came to shove that's who he chose to be with.'

Another little silence measured the seconds ticking by.

'About that transfer...' they said in unison.

'I'm OK about the transfer to the other unit,' Georgie said, lowering her gaze to stare at her hands twisting in her lap. 'I understand you don't want to work with me since...since we...you know...'

Ben got up from behind his desk and came to stand next to her chair. 'Georgie, look at me.'

She dragged her gaze upwards, two big tears already making their way down her cheeks, several others following their crystal pathway.

He reached out with the pad of his thumb and blotted them one by one. 'Why are you crying?' he asked, his voice sounding as if it had been scraped across a gravel road.

'B-because I stupidly fell in love with you,' she sobbed. 'Dumb, huh? I always do it. I fall in love with unavailable men. I never seem—'

'I'm not unavailable.'

'To learn from my past mist—' She stopped and blinked at him again. 'What did you say?'

'I'm not for a moment thinking of going back to Leila.'

Georgie swallowed the aching lump in her throat. 'You mean you're...you're not going to marry her?'

He shook his head. 'I don't love her. I don't think I ever did, to tell you the truth.'

She opened and closed her mouth, her toffee-brown eyes still looking up at him dazedly.

He pulled her to her feet and wrapping his arms around her brought her close. 'I want to be with you, Georgie, and only you,' he said. 'I knew I was in trouble the first day I met you which, when you think about it, was only nine or ten days ago, but as my mother always told me—when you meet the right person you just know.'

Georgie's heart began to race and her breathing halted as

she looked up into his earnest dark blue gaze. 'Do you mean the right person as in *the right* person?' she asked.

Ben smiled down at her. 'Yes. My father was the same when he met my mother. It must be genetic or something. I want you to be my wife. I love you. I fell for you when you knocked me off my bike, and I don't mean just onto the road. One look into those big brown eyes of yours and I was all wrapped up, but not just with bandages.'

'You really mean it?' she asked, her voice squeaking in surprise and joy.

'I adore you,' he said. 'I love everything about you. Your smile, that cute little nose of yours that tips up when you toss your head at me, your beautiful skin that felt so good next to mine. I could go on and on.'

'Go on,' she said, pressing herself closer to his hot, hard body.

His smile widened. 'I could go on all day but I want you to promise to be my wife first. I know I should really be asking your father first, and there are lots of other issues we have to deal with, but will you do it? Will you make me the happiest man alive by agreeing to marry me?'

She threw her arms around his neck and standing on tiptoe kissed him passionately all over his face. 'Yes, yes, yes, a thousand times…' Her face suddenly fell and she lowered her heels back to the floor. 'Uh-oh…'

He lifted one brow quizzically. 'Uh-oh?'

'Five thousand times uh-oh actually,' she amended with a rueful grimace.

'Five thousand, huh?' he said rubbing at his jaw. 'Now, that's totally spooky.'

Her eyes widened. 'It is?'

'Yep,' he said. 'I made this promise to Madeleine Brothers that if I dated another woman in the next six months I would donate five thousand dollars to the hospital research foundation.'

Georgie's eyes went even wider. 'I made the same promise to Rhiannon! Oh, my gosh, maybe Madame Celestia is the real deal after all.'

'You're surely not serious, sweetheart?' he asked with a tender look. 'You told me you didn't believe in all that stuff.'

She gave herself a mental shake and smiled up at him blissfully. 'The only thing I'm serious about is you, even if you're not blond.'

His eyes started to twinkle. 'Uh-oh.'

'Uh-oh here comes another uh-oh,' she said with a wry smile. 'What do you mean uh-oh?'

He released her for a moment to retrieve a family photograph sitting on his desk. He handed it to her without speaking.

Georgie looked down at the slightly faded photograph of a tall, dark-haired man who looked exactly like Ben, a petite woman who resembled Hannah standing by his side with a little baby boy with blond hair cradled in her arms.

Georgie looked up at Ben, a smile slowly spreading across her face. 'You were blond!' she said.

He grinned back at her. 'Yes, but only until I was six months old.'

She nestled closer to him again, her eyes shining with delight. 'So does this mean that any babies we have in the future will be the same?' she asked.

He pressed a kiss to the end of her uptilted nose. 'I guess we'll just have to wait and see,' he said, and smiled.

EPILOGUE

'So how's the morning sickness going?' Rhiannon asked a
Georgie sank into Rhiannon's leather sofa.

It had been a trying day, but had ended in joy. Not only wer
Georgie's final exams over but Emma Stanley had returned to
the hospital with baskets of chocolates for the staff to announce
that she had qualified for the national athletics squad. She had
recovered from Ben's surgery with minimal neurologica
deficit, and had been able to start training again within a couple
of months. After four years at the Institute of sport, her caree
now looked promising, her dreams and hopes restored.

'I'm feeling a bit better now my fellowship exams are
over,' Georgie answered. 'What a relief. Now I can concentrate on being barefoot and pregnant for a while. Ben's been
so good about holding off starting a family until I got my
exams finished. My dad thinks he's wonderful for being so
patient and supportive.'

'Wow, I never thought I'd hear you say that,' Rhiannon
said. 'I thought it was going to be daggers drawn at dawn
between them for the rest of your married life.'

Georgie smiled as she recalled Ben's first awkward visit
to her parents' home and how it had taken a few months to
melt the ice. 'I can't believe how well they get on these days,'

she said. 'Dad told Ben he always knew he was going to be a brilliant neurosurgeon but he felt Ben needed to sharpen his focus a little. It took a while for him to admit it but now Ben agrees with him. It was failing that exam that made him really hone his skills so that he would never doubt his ability in a crisis.'

'And, of course, your mum thinks her son-in-law is not only an extremely gifted neurosurgeon but the most romantic, gorgeous husband in the world,' Rhiannon commented.

Georgie smiled again and, placing her hand on her slightly rounded abdomen, moved it around in a gentle stroking motion. 'Mum's so excited about the baby,' she said. 'She's been knitting for four years in anticipation of this event and Hannah is already choosing names and laying bets on which one we'll use. We're down to her short list but it will be touch and go on who wins in the end.'

'Do you want to know the sex?' Rhiannon asked hopefully. 'I can always get Madame Celestia to do a prenatal reading for you.'

Georgie shook her head. 'I think I'll wait until our ultrasound tomorrow,' she said with another dreamy smile. 'I just love surprises.'

The next morning Ben and Georgie looked at the screen showing them the tiny heartbeat of their baby.

'Uh-oh,' they said in unison.

'That's not one baby,' the sonographer said somewhat unnecessarily. 'That's two. Congratulations. You're having twins.'

Ben and Georgie just looked at each other and smiled.

0408/03b

MILLS & BOON
MEDICAL™
On sale 2nd May 2008

THE OUTBACK DOCTOR'S SURPRISE BRIDE
by Amy Andrews

Dr James Remington soon settles into his new Outback community, especially when he meets nurse Helen Franklin. James never stays in one place for long, yet Helen makes James want something he's *never* wanted before: a home – and maybe even a family!

A WEDDING AT LIMESTONE COAST
by Lucy Clark

Working in A&E and her little twins keep single mum Stasy busy! Her bubbly exterior endears her to all – including her new boss Justin Gray. Single dad Justin realises that he has found his perfect family here in Limestone Coast – and longs to make Stasy his bride.

THE DOCTOR'S MEANT-TO-BE MARRIAGE
by Janice Lynn

Dr Chelsea Majors shared a kiss with Jared Floyd years ago, making her feel beautiful for the first time. Now they work together as GPs, Jared is as smouldering as ever, although there's a sadness in his eyes… Chelsea brings life and sparkle to the surgery, and the smile soon returns to Jared's chiselled face…

Available at WHSmith, Tesco, ASDA, and all good bookshops
www.millsandboon.co.uk

MILLS & BOON®

MEDICAL™

proudly presents

Brides of Penhally Bay

Featuring Dr Nick Tremayne

A pulse-raising collection of emotional, tempting romances and heart-warming stories – devoted doctors, single fathers, Mediterranean heroes, a sheikh and his guarded heart, royal scandals and miracle babies…

Book Five

THE DOCTOR'S ROYAL LOVE-CHILD

by Kate Hardy

on sale 4th April 2008

A COLLECTION TO TREASURE FOREVER!
One book available every month

MILLS & BOON

MEDICAL™

proudly presents

Brides of Penhally Bay

A pulse-raising collection of emotional,
tempting romances and heart-warming stories by
bestselling Mills & Boon® Medical™ authors

April 2008
The Doctor's Royal Love-Child
by Kate Hardy

There's a princess in Penhally!
HRH Melinda Fortesque comes to the Bay

May 2008
Nurse Bride, Bayside Wedding
by Gill Sanderson

Edward Tremayne finds the woman of his dreams...

June 2008
Single Dad Seeks a Wife
by Melanie Milburne

Meet hunky Penhally Bay Chief Inspector Lachlan D'Ancey
and his search for love.

*Let us whisk you away to an idyllic Cornish town –
a place where hearts are made whole*

COLLECT ALL 12 BOOKS!

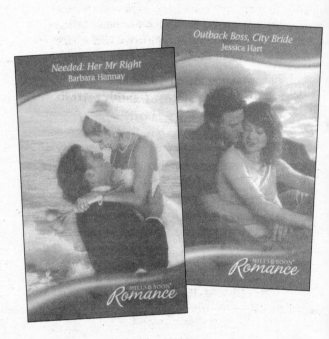

Celebrate 100 years of pure reading pleasure with Mills & Boon®

To mark our centenary, each month we're publishing a special 100th Birthday Edition. These celebratory editions are packed with extra features and include a FREE bonus story.

Plus, starting in February you'll have the chance to enter a fabulous monthly prize draw. See 100th Birthday Edition books for details.

Now that's worth celebrating!

15th February 2008

Raintree: Inferno by Linda Howard
Includes FREE bonus story Loving Evangeline
A double dose of Linda Howard's heady mix of passion and adventure

4th April 2008

The Guardian's Forbidden Mistress by Miranda Lee
Includes FREE bonus story The Magnate's Mistress
Two glamorous and sensual reads from favourite author Miranda Lee!

2nd May 2008

The Last Rake in London by Nicola Cornick
Includes FREE bonus story The Notorious Lord
Lose yourself in two tales of high society and rakish seduction!

Look for Mills & Boon 100th Birthday Editions at your favourite bookseller or visit
www.millsandboon.co.uk

4 FREE

BOOKS AND A SURPRISE GIFT!

We would like to take this opportunity to thank you for reading this Mills & Boon® book by offering you the chance to take FOUR more specially selected titles from the Medical™ series absolutely FREE! We're also making this offer to introduce you to the benefits of the Mills & Boon® Reader Service™—

- ★ FREE home delivery
- ★ FREE gifts and competitions
- ★ FREE monthly Newsletter
- ★ Exclusive Reader Service offers
- ★ Books available before they're in the shops

Accepting these FREE books and gift places you under no obligation to buy, you may cancel at any time, even after receiving your free shipment. Simply complete your details below and return the entire page to the address below. You don't even need a stamp!

YES! Please send me 4 free Medical books and a surprise gift. I understand that unless you hear from me, I will receive 6 superb new titles every month for just £2.99 each, postage and packing free. I am under no obligation to purchase any books and may cancel my subscription at any time. The free books and gift will be mine to keep in any case.

M8ZED

Ms/Mrs/Miss/Mr ....Initials ....
BLOCK CAPITALS PLEASE

Surname ....

Address ....

....

....Postcode............................

Send this whole page to:
UK: FREEPOST CN81, Croydon, CR9 3WZ